Our story begins with Jason, a brave, smart young hero and the future king of a land named Iolcus. Unfortunately, his cunning uncle Pelias stole his throne. But Jason's destiny was prophesied by an oracle: He would bring about his power-hungry uncle's doom. So, Pelias set his nephew forth on an impossible quest, far too treacherous for any mortal—to find the priceless and powerful Golden Fleece.

Everyone knows that a truly great quest requires a courageous hero. Meet Zeus, a tiny little hamster with a mighty appetite for power. His cage sits atop a high shelf at Mount Olympus Pet Center, so he can watch over his kingdom below. Being king of the gods is a tough job: You've got to issue orders and decrees, make sure to stay in tip-top shape by running on your exercise wheel, and most importantly, lead your minions on epic journeys. And Zeus the Mighty has one giant task in front of him: Find the "golden fleas" and solidify his position before the other gods rebel.

With every misstep, misunderstanding, and gut-busting gaffe along the way, this quirky new take on Greek mythology combines humor, animals, and adventure in a tale that will have kids of all ages rolling on the floor laughing. And if that isn't enough, "The Truth Behind the Fiction" section of the book reveals fascinating details of the original myth, plus history and information about the Greek world. With a unique mix of adorable illustrations, witty dialogue, and mystifying mythology, *Zeus the Mighty* entertains, inspires, and informs.

Onward, Argonauts!

Jennifer Emmett

Jennifer Emmett, Senior Vice President, National Geographic Kids Media

MAJOR NATIONAL MARKETING CAMPAIGN

Publicity
- Prepublication industry buzz and early adopter campaign
- National broadcast, print, and digital media
- Selected author events
- Major laydown of advance reader's copies and chapter samplers

Advertising & Consumer Promotion
- National consumer print, digital, and video platform advertising to parents and kids
- Promotion across National Geographic media and consumer venues
- Book giveaway promotion in 20 major radio markets
- Attention-grabbing promotion at consumer cons and events
- Major social media promotion across all platforms
- Lively, broadcast-ready book trailer

Library & Education
- Major promotion at national school and library conferences
- In-school marketing targeting teachers and students
- Print advertising in library and education media
- Educator's guide with downloadable classroom activities

zeusthemighty.com

Series Title:	Zeus the Mighty
Title (Book 1):	The Quest for the Golden Fleas
Author:	Crispin Boyer
Illustrator:	Andy Elkerton
Publisher:	National Geographic
Imprint:	Under the Stars
Publication Date:	October 22, 2019
Format:	Hardcover, Paper Over Board
Trim:	5-1/2 x 8-1/4
Pages:	192
Illustrations:	black-and-white throughout
BISAC:	JUV001000 JUVENILE FICTION / Animals – Mice, Hamsters, Guinea Pigs
	JUV067000 JUVENILE FICTION / Legends, Myths, Fables – Greek & Roman
	JUV035000 JUVENILE FICTION / Animals - Pets
ISBN:	978-1-4263 -3547-1
Price:	$12.99/$17.99 CAN
GLB ISBN:	978-1-4263-3548-8
GLB Price:	$22.90/$29.90 CAN
E-book ISBN:	978-1-4263-3549-5
E-book Price:	$7.99/$17.99 CAN
Ages:	8-12

Please refer any questions or reviews of this book to:
Media Masters Publicity
61 Depot Street
Tryon, NC 28782
tracey@mmpublicity.com

THE MIGHTY

The Quest for the Golden Fleas

CRISPIN BOYER

Illustrated by Andy Elkerton

UNDER THE Stars

NATIONAL GEOGRAPHIC

Since 1888, the National Geographic Society has funded more than 12,000 research, exploration, and preservation projects around the world. The Society receives funds from National Geographic Partners, LLC, funded in part by your purchase. A portion of the proceeds from this book supports this vital work. To learn more, visit natgeo.com/info.

NATIONAL GEOGRAPHIC and Yellow Border Design are trademarks of the National Geographic Society, used under license.

For more information, visit nationalgeographic.com, call 1-800-647-5463, or write to the following address:

National Geographic Partners
1145 17th Street N.W.
Washington, D.C. 20036-4688 U.S.A.

Visit us online at nationalgeographic.com/books

For librarians and teachers: ngchildrensbooks.org

More for kids from National Geographic: natgeokids.com

For information about special discounts for bulk purchases, please contact National Geographic Books Special Sales: specialsales@natgeo.com

For rights or permissions inquiries, please contact National Geographic Books Subsidiary Rights: bookrights@natgeo.com

Designed by Amanda Larsen
Hand-Lettering by Jay Roeder

Hardcover ISBN: 978-1-4263-3547-1
Reinforced library binding ISBN: 978-1-4263-3548-8

On sale: 10/22/19 * Ages 8-12 * Territory: World except United Kingdom, Ireland, Channel Islands, Isle of Man, Australia, New Zealand, Sweden, Denmark, Norway, Finland, Japan, India, Bangladesh, Bhutan, Maldives, Nepal, Pakistan and Sri Lanka * 192 pages * 5-1/2 x 8-1/4 * Carton Quantity: 12 * Category: Juvenile * ISBN (hardcover) 978-1-4263-3547-1 * $12.99 US/$17.99 CAN * ISBN (reinforced library binding) 978-1-4263-3548-8 * $22.90 US/$29.90 CAN

ARC contents not final. For promotion only.

DEDICATION

ART TO COME
Map of Pet Center

ART TO COME
Map of Pet Center

PREFACE

ARTEMIS AMBROSIA WAS BEING WATCHED.
She sensed it as she went about her evening routine closing up Mount Olympus Pet Center, topping off bowls of Mutt Nuggets, organizing a display of cat-scratching posts, testing the algae levels in the fish tanks to make sure the water was just right.

Artemis—or "Artie" for short—knew who was doing the watching. It wasn't cat or dog or reptile or fish eyes she felt boring into the back of her head. "Okay, what is it, buddy?" she asked, spinning to face the golden hamster watching her from his cage high above the cash register.

"If I didn't know any better," Artie said, walking toward the hamster, "I'd suspect you're waiting for me to leave so you can sneak out on another misadventure." She reached up and stuck a finger through the bars to scratch at a patch of white fur on the hamster's cheek. Then she tugged firmly on the cage door. "Not tonight, my little escape artist!" she said, satisfied that it was locked tight.

The hamster gave a little squeak, and Artie grinned. As much as she loved animals, she didn't actually speak hamster. Or dog, or cat, or fish, or even cricket for that matter. If she did, she would know a lot more took place in her pet center than she believed.

Artie took a final lap around the room. She checked to make sure the lid on the bug house was snug. She shook a few more flakes of fish food into the tanks. She stopped by the kennels along the big front picture window and reached down to scratch an orange tabby curled up in a cat bed. Finally, she zipped up her jacket and switched off the lights, plunging the room into the dim red glow of the large Mount Olympus Pet Center sign.

As she opened the front door, Artie glanced back at her favorite rescued rodent. "Nighty night, Zeus the Mighty." She blew him a kiss. "I better not find you in a weird place in the morning." She pulled the door shut—then immediately reopened it and pointed at her hamster. "I mean it, Zeus—stay put!"

Somewhere nearby, probably in the bug bin, a cricket chirped loudly. Artie closed the door and locked it.

CHAPTER 1

ZEUS THE MIGHTY DIPPED HIS TOE INTO THE RAGING WHIRLPOOL. "Eeek!" he squeaked. "The water's too wet! Lift me, Demeter! Get me out of here!"

Zeus clung to a long, skinny arm of his cricket friend Demeter, dangling from a narrow ridge above the swirling waters. "What's the matter, Zeus?" Demeter hollered down. "You see the monster?"

"Just pull me up!" Zeus shouted. "Now!"

"Oh, okay, you got it!" Demeter yanked her arm upward so quickly that Zeus nearly lost his grip. But he managed to scramble up the whirlpool's smooth white surface and onto the ridge beside Demeter. While Zeus caught his breath, Demeter peeked at the whooshing waters below.

"Sorry about that," she said. "You know sea monsters make me jumpy ever since that whole Atlantis fiasco."

"What do you have to be nervous about?" Zeus asked, still panting. "I'm the one doing all the heavy lifting here."

Demeter looked confused and shook out an arm. "Mmm, I dunno. I wouldn't exactly call you light."

"I don't mean, like, literally heavy lifting," Zeus shot back. "What I'm saying is, being king of the gods isn't easy. A lot of late nights. A lot of sleepless days.

"Speaking of which," Demeter looked around. "What time is it? I feel like Artie said goodnight ages ago."

Zeus pressed on. "Planning all our adventures. Protecting the kingdom. Putting up with Poseidon's lip. It's exhausting!"

"I hear ya," Demeter said in her soothing tone. She nibbled from the strip of lettuce she wore across her shoulder, an ever-present snack to satisfy her bottomless insect appetite.

"But, it's a job I don't take lightly. I mean … sometimes I think, why, why me?"

"I'm sure Poseidon would love to fill in for a bit if you wanted a vacation," Demeter began.

"Do I look like I need a vacation?"

Zeus stood to his full six inches and puffed out his chest. The golden fur on his head stuck in all directions above his laurel-wreath crown, and the patch of white hair on his cheek quivered. Demeter had once told him she thought the patch looked like a storm cloud when Zeus got riled up. She used it to forecast his mood, and right now his mood was not good. Demeter was eager to change the subject. "So is Charybdis really lurking down in that whirlpool?"

"Actually, Charybdis *is* the whirlpool."

"Huh?" Demeter spit bits of lettuce. She stared into the watery cavern of the white porcelain basin with a small black hole at the center. She watched as water swirled around the edges. "You sure he's down there, boss?"

"He's not a very sophisticated monster," Zeus said. "He just kinda spends all day sucking in water to make whirlpools. Did I mention Charybdis is mostly mouth?"

"If you're trying to make me less nervous, it's not working." Demeter swallowed loudly. "There's no chance it might be some other sea monster down there? Typhon maybe?"

"Typhon?" Zeus scoffed. "He's not a sea monster. Plus, he's out of the picture. I sealed him away in that volcano, remember? It was kind of a big deal. I'm pretty famous for it."

"Oh, duh," Demeter said, slapping her forehead. "You're right, Zeus."

"Of course I'm right! Whirlpools are Charybdis's thing. All the signs are obvious. Like, literally." Zeus jabbed his thumb over his shoulder at a white sign hanging high above them. It featured a crude image of two soapy hands clasped together under a running faucet, but to Zeus, it looked *exactly* like a sea monster with a wide-open mouth. Beneath it was a series of letters that might as well have been Greek.

EMPLOYEES MUST
WASH HANDS BEFORE
RETURNING TO WORK

ART NOT FINAL

Demeter squinted at the sign. "What's it say?"

"Who cares? The picture's what's important: Giant mouth. Whirlpool. That's Charybdis, all right. He's down there!"

Demeter looked at the raging waters and shuddered. "That beast's famous for more than whirlpools. I remember all the stories you told me, Zeus, about how Charybdis swallows ships whole."

"Which is exactly why we need to kick him out of Greece!" Zeus said. "To save our ships!"

"Shouldn't we have maybe asked Poseidon along for this adventure?" Demeter said. "He *is* the lord of water."

"I don't need that snobby pufferfish's permission! I rule all of Greece! That includes the sea!!"

"Right, right, of course." Demeter held up her arms. "I just thought if we're really going to try to get rid of a ship-swallowing whirlpool monster, it might be nice to have Poseidon around. You know, for backup."

"You don't need backup when you're *me*," Zeus said, pounding his chest. "And besides, can you imagine the look on Poseidon's face when he hears we kicked this monster from his own backyard without his help? He won't be so

puffed up then!"

Demeter's eyes narrowed. "I thought we were doing this to save Greece?"

Zeus ignored her. "The question is, how do we kick Charybdis out? I'd do it myself, but I'd get all pruny." He held up his paws and wriggled his fingers.

"That sounds awful."

"You don't even know. I suppose I could whip up some lightning bolts and give Charybdis a real shock … but that seems kinda showy."

"Showy is good." Demeter nodded. "I like showy."

"Nah, too cliché. Sealing up the volcano worked for Typhon," Zeus said, reflecting on his long-ago triumph over his chief foe. "Maybe we can do the same trick with Charybdis here?" Zeus rubbed his fuzzy chin and looked around the rim of the whirlpool. He spotted a shiny metal bar sticking out of the white cliff face above them. "Up there!" Zeus pointed. "Demeter, gimme a boost!"

Demeter hunched down to let Zeus use her like a step. "Oof. Ow. Pretty sure … this is heavy lifting … but whatever," she muttered as the king of the gods clambered onto her back. His weight smooshed her flat, but she managed to give Zeus just enough of a boost to grip the metal bar. Its end dipped slightly.

"I thought so!" Zeus shouted as he pulled himself to a seated position, sitting on the bar like a bench. "This thing is stuck in the cliff here. If I yank it out, I bet I could bring the whole wall here down onto the whirlpool! That would trap Charybdis for good!"

Beneath Zeus, Demeter scrambled back to her feet and backed away. "Uh, great idea, boss. I'll just give you some room to do your thing."

"I *only* have great ideas." Zeus stood on the bar and jumped, making it jiggle. "See, buddy? This wall will come down in no time. Do I know how to seal away a monster or what?"

"Oh, yeah. This is becoming, like, your signature move."

"Well, let's not get crazy. I know lots of other moves." Zeus leapt again with more force. The bar jiggled more violently.

A sudden calm descended across the waters. Both Demeter and Zeus looked down to see that the whirlpool had stopped swirling.

"Oh no. Did you scare Charybdis away?" Demeter's

ART NOT FINAL

disappointment didn't sound genuine.

"No, no, quite the opposite. He's just trying to make us think that. He wants us to hop in the water so he can swallow us down in one big gulp. That is *classic* Charybdis!"

"Hah! Not falling for it, monster!" Demeter taunted the whirlpool as Zeus began bouncing with gusto on the metal bar. Its tip dipped deeply beneath his weight.

"Almost there!" Zeus said, panting. "It's getting looser!"

Blub-blub-blub! Bubbles roiled from below the water's calm surface.

"Oh, you were so right, Zeus!" Demeter shouted. "He's still down there!"

The bar continued to dip beneath Zeus's feet, threatening to spill him off. "Whoa!" He hugged the cool white surface of the cliff face to keep from slipping.

Glub-glub-glub. More bubbles broke the surface, accompanied by a rushing sound from deep below. Demeter craned her head over the edge.

"I'm ... I'm slipping!" Zeus squeaked as he slid down and off the bar. He made a frantic grab for its tip and latched on with one paw, yanking the bar downward.

FLOOSH! The rushing grew into a roar beneath the water, which spun into a whirlpool more ferocious than before, circling toward the center of the dark pit.

"Whoa!" Demeter stared at the center of the whirlpool, unaware of Zeus hanging by one paw above her.

Zeus's grip slipped. He tumbled, falling past Demeter. "Help!" he yelled.

Startled, Demeter reached out and grabbed Zeus as he plummeted past. "No! Your paws will get pruny!" she called. But Zeus's momentum pulled Demeter off the slippery surface of the ridge, and together they fell into the whirlpool of the ship-swallowing monster.

CHAPTER 2

SPLASH!

"Eeek!" Zeus shouted, helpless against the fearsome tug of the whirlpool. "It's sucking me down!"

Demeter paddled more easily against the current and reached out to grab her friend. "I'll get you, Zeus!"

A shadow fell across the whirlpool, and Zeus looked up. He saw a head wearing a bronze Spartan war helmet, with its fearsome mask and plume of brushy black fur sprouting out of the top. Much of the face within the helmet was hidden, but Zeus could see a pink tongue and the figure's spiky collar, just visible above the ridge.

"Heya, guys," the head within the helmet said cheerfully, giving a quick nod. The helmet slid back, revealing the

wrinkled face of a pug beneath the visor. "Going for a swim?"

Zeus splashed and sputtered. "Does it look like I'm going for a swim, Ares?! Get me out of here!"

"What are you drooling on now, war god?" Another fuzzy head appeared alongside the pug. It belonged to a tabby cat whose face was framed by a mane of wiry orange hair kept slightly under control by a golden laurel wreath atop her head. Around her neck she wore a gold collar, from which dangled a crystal charm shaped like an owl. Delicate golden bracelets wound around her forepaws, which were propped against the ridge. Her amber eyes seemed to triple in size at the sight of a hamster and cricket swirling around the whirlpool below. "Zeus!" the cat exclaimed. "Demeter! That's a foolish place for a swim!"

"We're not swimming!" the hamster and cricket yelled at the same time.

Zeus had drifted dangerously close to the center of the whirlpool—and Charybdis's massive mouth. Demeter swam alongside Zeus and tried to wrap her front legs around her hamster friend. "A little help, Athena?" she called to the cat.

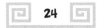

Ares the pug had leapt back from the edge of the whirlpool and was running in circles, a blur of tan fur. "We're going swimming! We're going swimming!" Then he stopped and began scratching an ear beneath his helmet.

Athena reached down with a paw and scooped Zeus out before all the water was swallowed down with a *glug-glug-glug*. "I got ya!" Demeter latched onto Athena's furry arm and clung tight. The cat deposited them both on the smooth white ridge above the mostly-empty basin.

Demeter hopped on one leg and pounded on the side of her head with her two right arms, shaking droplets of water from her long dark antennae and the gold laurel wreath on her head. She sniffed at the soggy lettuce sash she wore over her shoulder. It clearly didn't smell right, because she ripped the sash loose and tossed it into the basin.

Zeus lay on his belly and wheezed. His golden fur, normally silky soft, was now sopping wet but his clothes were as dry and spotless as ever.

He used a paw to push the wet fur out of his eyes and noticed that the basin of the whirlpool was refilling with

water. Charybdis was nowhere to be seen.

Demeter looked up at Athena, who was licking droplets from one furry bracelet-wrapped paw. "Good thing you showed up when you did," Demeter said. "One more spin around and we would've would up in the belly of the whirlpool monster!"

"Monster?!" Ares jostled Athena as he propped his front paws on the ridge to rejoin the group. With a body stockier than most pugs, he looked a lot like a meat loaf with legs and a curly tail. "Which kind of monster?!"

"The whirlpool kind," Demeter said. "You know, Charybdis."

"Charybdis?!" Athena repeated, her eyes shining. "You found that ship-swallowing beast and didn't tell us other  Olympians? Why didn't you ask us for help? We're supposed to be a team!"

Zeus got to his feet and shook off his damp fur. "I didn't need any help, Athena. As you can see, Charybdis is gone."

The three Olympians peered into the whirlpool basin, which now held calm and clear water.

Athena said, "Are you sure Charybdis was ever really there to begin wi—"

"He's gone!" Zeus repeated. "Defeated. Sent packing. Never to swallow a ship again. Thanks to Zeus the Mighty. Me. King of the gods. And with zero help from anyone, especially Poseidon!"

"Poseidon?" Athena muttered, turning to Ares. "Did you bring up Poseidon?"

The pug shook his head, spraying Athena with drool.

"Maybe you had a little help from your super-duper adventure partner, best pal, and number one minion?" Demeter asked in a hopeful tone.

Zeus considered Demeter's words for a moment. "Sure, pal, I'll give you an assist on this."

"YESSS!" Demeter pumped four cricket arms in the air.

Zeus inspected his fingers for wrinkles. "Everyone give yourself a hand for being here to witness my fearlessness and courage and bravery and so on and so forth."

Demeter applauded four arms eagerly. Ares wagged his

tail. Athena sort of nodded, mostly to shake Ares's drool from her fur.

"So, uh, why did you guys wander in here, anyway?" Demeter asked Athena and Ares.

"I was thirsty," Ares said. He stretched his neck into the basin—nearly crushing Zeus and Demeter with his spiked collar—and stuck out his tongue just long enough to lap water from the bowl.

"Eeeww." Demeter wrinkled her face. "I'm not sure you should be drinking that. I mean, it just had a whirlpool monster living in it."

Splish-splish-splish. "Yummy," the pug said between laps. His helmet had slid back down over his face, so only his tongue was visible poking between the cheek guards.

"And I'm here because ... well ..." Athena trailed off.

"Well what?" Demeter asked.

"I need to, you know ... go," Athena answered.

"Ooh, where you going?" Ares asked, coming up for air. Demeter's discarded strip of lettuce hung from his nose. "Can I come, too?"

"Ares! No! I mean, I need to *go.*" Athena pointed a paw toward a sandy patch behind the whirlpool's base. "So if you all wouldn't mind …"

"I don't mind, buddy," Ares said. "Do your thing." He dipped his dripping face back into the water for another round.

Athena stared at Zeus and Demeter.

"Yeah, no, we should go," Zeus said, tugging on Ares's collar. The pug didn't budge.

A familiar voice rang out in the distance. "Ares? Ares! Who's a good boy? Who wants to go outside?!" The pug immediately spun around, nearly yanking Zeus off the ridge.

"Ooh, ooh, ooh, I'm a good boy, Artie!" he shouted. Ares ran off, Demeter's soggy lettuce dangling from his nose.

"Artie's out there?" Zeus asked, concern in his voice. "Gosh, what time is it?"

"Noon, maybe," Athena said, then sighed in relief. "I'm just glad Artie's here to call off Ares. He was *not* getting the hint." The tabby lifted Zeus and then Demeter off the porcelain ridge, setting them gently on the ground. "Now if you both don't mind, a little privacy, please?"

"Sure, Athena," Zeus said.

"Yeah," Demeter agreed. "Like Ares said, you do your thing."

Zeus and Demeter scurried after Ares, leaving Athena, goddess of wisdom, to take care of her urgent business.

CHAPTER 3

ZEUS AND DEMETER FOLLOWED ARES, watching until the pug had squeezed through the dog-size portal to the airy northern land, where Ares, Athena, and the other large animals went to stretch their legs.

"Attaboy, Ares," said a tall redheaded woman who stepped into view in front of Mount Olympus. "You're really getting the hang of your doggy door!"

"Uh-oh," Zeus said, pulling Demeter to a sudden stop. "Artie's blocking the way home."

To Zeus and the other Olympians, Artie was their caretaker. She looked after all the inhabitants of land, sea, and air, cleaning their living quarters, making sure the food

was plentiful, and dealing with the other humans who frequently visited Greece. Artie wore her long hair in a ponytail so it wouldn't catch on chamber doors or dip into the sea as she went about her duties. She dressed plainly, in denim jeans and a shirt emblazoned with an image of Mount Olympus seared by a thunderbolt. Her pockets always packed treats of every sort. The animals loved her, but they also tried to stay out of her way. The few times she caught them going about their adventures, she did not seem pleased.

"Last thing we need is Artie finding us out and about," Demeter said. "I heard her warning about staying away from weird places last night." She looked up at Mount Olympus, where she lived with Zeus, then unfurled one of her tiny wings and gave it a wiggle. "I'd just fly us both home if I could, but these wings aren't built for heavy lifting."

"Knock it off with the heavy lifting," Zeus said absentmindedly. He peered into the late-afternoon haze, looking eastward across Greece, which stretched almost as far as he could see, to the edge of the Aegean Sea. Poseidon's realm. "It'll take us forever to hike the long way around the sea," he said.

"And you don't need Poseidon seeing you hoof it home," Demeter said. "He'll do anything to make you look bad. It's like he doesn't know you're the boss of him!"

Zeus changed the subject. "We need a distraction."

Almost as if on cue, familiar harp music began playing from the direction of Mount Olympus. Zeus looked up to see Artie fiddling with the rectangular black device she carried with her everywhere. Sometimes the device played music or flashed images. The Olympians all suspected it was enchanted, activated by whatever complex spells Artie traced with her fingers across its flat surface. She tapped her finger on the sleek rectangle, and the harp music got louder. Then it faded as a woman's voice began speaking: "Welcome to Greeking Out, your weekly podcast that delivers the goods on Greek gods and epic tales of triumphant heroes. I'm your host, the Oracle of Wi-Fi."

ART TO COME

"Yes!" Zeus exclaimed.

"No!" Demeter shot back. "The Oracle's about to start and we're stuck out here! We'll miss the important bits!"

When Artie summoned *Greeking Out* on her device each week, the Olympians listened carefully. The Oracle was like a teacher and fortune-teller combined, often providing hints about their next adventure.

"This is the distraction we need," Zeus said. "You know Artie always loses herself in her chores when the Oracle gets rolling. She'll never notice us sneaking back to Mount Olympus." Zeus huddled with Demeter and kept his eye on Artie, who was still examining her device. "Get ready to make a run for it."

"This week," the Oracle continued, "I shall tell you all about Jason and the Argonauts."

"Jason and the who-gonauts?" Demeter whispered.

"Shhh." Zeus put a finger to Demeter's mouth. "Watch Artie!"

Artie set the device down on a foothill beneath Mount Olympus and picked up her basket. It held the cleaning brushes, bins of food, and other tools of her caretaking trade—everything she needed to complete her long daily ritual of tending Zeus's kingdom.

"Coast is clear," Zeus whispered. "Last one home drinks Poseidon's helmet water!"

The hamster and cricket sprinted in the direction of Mount Olympus. Demeter, as always, easily outpaced Zeus with her mighty leaps. "Aw, c'mon," Zeus panted, "wait up."

"Sorry, Zeus!" Demeter said. "You know I only got one speed!"

"Today's tale involves a dashing hero, a crew of brave sailors, a fearsome dragon, a mysterious land, and a quest for a powerful treasure: the Golden Fleece."

"This sounds like a good one," Demeter said.

Zeus caught up with Demeter outside the glass walls of the Bugcropolis, the box-shaped city of insects near Mount Olympus. Crickets, grasshoppers, hissing cockroaches, and other leggy creatures all cheered and waved at Demeter as she paused before her hometown. She was the goddess of the harvest and their most famous resident. One particularly loud hissing cockroach reached a scrawny arm through a hole in the city's roof and tossed Demeter a fresh strip of lettuce. She snatched it from the air and tied it into a new sash before bowing in gratitude.

"Show off to your followers later," Zeus said, slapping the cricket on her back as he ran past. "We're almost home. I don't want to miss another word of the Oracle's teachings!"

Demeter gave one more bow to her followers, then leapt out in front of Zeus. "One step ahead of ya, boss!"

"Now sit back and heed the Oracle's words, listeners, as I breathe new life into one of the earliest stories ever written. A glimpse of how the ancient Greeks saw their world. A tale told and retold for three thousand years."

"Blah, blah, blah," Zeus muttered. "Get to the good stuff!"

Demeter was just steps from the rope that she and Zeus used to climb to the peak of Mount Olympus, when she skidded to a halt. Before her stood the mouth of a big black cave, one she had never seen before. Its entrance was sealed with a sturdy metal grate. The cave appeared to be carved from black rock. "Where'd this come from?" Demeter leaned in to inspect it.

"Don't know! Keep moving!" Zeus shouted as he jogged past.

Demeter ignored Zeus and poked her head through the cold metal bars of the grate, peering into the darkness.

Just when she decided there was nothing inside, two golden slits, shaped like reptilian eyes, pierced the inky blackness. A wet gust of smelly air wafted from the depths as a skinny tongue flicked at Demeter's chest. "Aieee!" she screeched, leaping toward Zeus and sending him sprawling. They landed in a heap next to their climbing rope.

Artie looked up from scrubbing the side of a fish tank. "Someone get loose over there?"

"Stay still!" Zeus wrapped his arms around

ART TO COME

Demeter, who had her eyes locked on the gated mouth of the cave behind them. Nothing stirred inside.

Artie headed slowly toward Mount Olympus. The only sound now was the voice of the Oracle. "This episode of *Greeking Out* is brought to you by Mutt Nuggets, tasty treats made with only the finest meats for all good doggos!"

"Someone say Mutt Nuggets?!" Ares barked, materializing through his portal.

"Ares!" Artie said. "You finished with your business outside?"

Ares barked, then slipped and scrambled his way to his chambers.

Artie watched him plop down in his kennel at the front of the pet center. She pulled a handful of Mutt Nuggets from her shirt pocket to reward the plump pug for his number two, and made him give her a "high five" before relinquishing the treats. Glancing back to the rear of the pet center, she saw her favorite hamster watching her through the bars of his cage on the shelf above the store counter. Noticing nothing amiss, Artie shrugged and returned to her cleaning.

Zeus and Demeter collapsed, exhausted, into the sweet-smelling cedar chips that lined the floor of Zeus's palace. Thanks to Ares, they had scrambled up their rope to the top of Mount Olympus unnoticed, then squeezed into the palace through its hidden back gate. They were winded, but safe from being caught by Artie—and just in time to hear the Oracle's tale of Jason and the Argonauts.

CHAPTER 4

FROM HIS PALACE ATOP MOUNT OLYMPUS, Zeus could see his fellow Olympians settling in for the Oracle's lesson. There was Ares scarfing down some treats in his chambers to the south. Far to the east, across mountains, plains, and sea, Zeus saw Athena, wisest of the gods, curled in her bed and using a paw to clean the tufts of orange fur at the tips of her ears. In the center of it all was the Aegean Sea, currently being tended by Artie. Zeus couldn't think of a better caretaker for his realm. He thought he could spot Poseidon the pufferfish gliding beneath the waves of the Aegean, no doubt lording over his fish minions. "All of this is mine," Zeus muttered to himself, a frequent habit when he was thinking. "Even if I

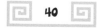

don't know what lies beyond …." Zeus eyed the portal that marked the edge of the Olympians' known world.

"Our story begins with Jason," the Oracle continued. "He was a handsome, brave, wise young hero."

"Like me," Zeus whispered. He gazed around his palace, looking past his exercise wheel, over his cushy round bed, until his gaze settled on the upside-down bottle that Artie kept filled with drinking water on the opposite wall. He walked to the bottle and examined his reflection in it, admiring the way his amber fur seemed to glow with an inner light that outshone even his gilded laurel-wreath crown and the golden thunderbolt emblem on his chest. The fabric of his royal chiton always fell just right, never wrinkling or ripping, never becoming stinky or stained. Like all Olympian attire, it was enchanted, indestructible, waterproof, and always comfy, like pj's made of mist. Divine duds were just another perk of the Olympian lifestyle.

"Jason wasn't your average ancient Greek hero," the Oracle went on. "He was also a king—or he was supposed to be. Jason's power-hungry uncle, Pelias, had stolen Jason's throne …."

"Oh, I can relate," Zeus muttered. "Poseidon's always

challenging my authority, too. Right, buddy?" Zeus asked Demeter, who was crouched at the columns of the palace. But her eyes were locked on the creepy crate far below. "Hey, you okay over there?" Zeus asked. Demeter just nibbled at her lettuce sash.

"Jason traveled to his uncle's palace to confront him ..."

"Yeah, you show him who's boss, Jason," Zeus muttered. His eyelids began to droop. Between his dip in the whirlpool and the panicked sprint home, the little hamster was pooped. He plopped down in his exercise wheel, letting the Oracle's story wash over him.

ART TO COME

"Pelias was prepared for his nephew's visit. Just as you have me as your oracle, faithful listener, Pelias had his own wise adviser and teller of truths. And his oracle issued to him frightful news: Jason would bring about his doom. So King Pelias came up with a cunning plan to rid himself of his nephew. He posed to the young man an impossible challenge. 'You want your kingdom'"—the Oracle's voice deepened as she impersonated Pelias—"'you must find me the Golden Fleece.'"

"Golden Fleas?" Zeus muttered. The thought made the white patch on his cheek itch. He scratched at it in his half sleep.

"This was a trap," the Oracle explained. "Pelias knew the quest for the Golden Fleece—a priceless treasure and powerful artifact—was far too dangerous for any mortal. But Jason was fearless and brimming with confidence. If anyone could find the Golden Fleece, it was him. He would use his uncle's trick against him. If Jason retrieved the treasure for his uncle, then his uncle would be forced to acknowledge Jason's authority. The Golden Fleece was the key to Jason's kingdom."

The words jolted Zeus awake. He leapt from the wheel and began sprinting around his palace. "I gotta get these fleas! I gotta get these fleas!"

His outburst startled Demeter from her vigil over the cave. "You gotta get *fleas*?" she asked.

Zeus scrambled back to his exercise wheel. "Not any fleas, Demeter. *Golden* Fleas! Didn't you hear the Oracle? The Golden Fleas are the keys to the kingdom! If I find them, then Poseidon would have to admit I'm the king of all of Greece. No more lip from that stuffy pufferfish!"

"You know, some of my best friends in the Bugcropolis are fleas. Don't recall knowing any golden ones, though—"

"Hush!" Zeus held up a paw. "Oracle's talking."

Beneath them, the teachings continued. "Jason was confident but not foolish. He knew he couldn't retrieve the Golden Fleece on his own, so to help him, the goddess Athena built a magical boat, called the Argo, and filled it with a who's who of Greek heroes, called the Argonauts."

"Athena can build boats?" Demeter asked.

"Shhh," hissed Zeus.

"The Argonauts sailed over the edge of the known world, into uncharted territory, to find the Fleece ..." Zeus peered across Greece again, wondering where he might find this "uncharted territory."

"In their travels, they encountered Phineus, a famous

soothsayer. Soothsayers were important people in ancient Greece because they could foresee events. Yet while Phineus could see the future, he couldn't see the present. The gods had blinded him because he was such a know-it-all. They sent winged Harpies to devour his food before he could eat a morsel. Jason knew if he saved Phineus, the soothsayer would help him find the Fleece. So Jason hatched a plan—"

"Ding-dong, anyone home?" Someone opened the main portal to Mount Olympus Pet Center. The animals looked up to see a wiry woman with short sandy hair carrying a bulging bag enter their realm. "Who's ready to make a mess?" she called as the portal shut behind her.

CHAPTER 5

"CALLIE!" ARTIE SHOUTED, RACING TO HER DEVICE TO PAUSE THE ORACLE'S STORY.** "You're ..." She looked at the device's screen. "You're right on time!" She crossed to the front door, flipping the Open sign to Closed. "We're closing up early today, everyone." The red letters that spelled out "Mount Olympus Pet Center" in the shop's picture window stayed lit. At night, they made the perfect night-light for the animals.

Artie shook Callie's hand, then swept an arm in front of her. "Welcome to Mount Olympus Pet Center, soon to be the most popular pet-adoption center in Athens, Georgia—with your help."

"That's the plan," said Artie's friend.

"Let me introduce you to the zoo." Artemis cleared her throat. "Hear ye, hear ye, denizens of Mount Olympus." The Olympians and other animals watched silently. "May I present Callista of Callista's Construction Company."

"Um, hi." Callista waved. "My friends call me Callie."

The animals looked at her.

"Huh," Callie said. "I dunno if they like me."

"Oh, they will once they get to know you," Artie said. "And you'll just love them. You'll see. You'll be spending a lot of time with them. Or at least next door to them."

"What's Artie talking about?" Zeus asked Demeter. "Who is this human?"

"I … I dunno," Demeter said. "I guess she lives here now?"

"Well, she can't live up here." Zeus crossed his arms. "We were just about to learn how to save Fingus from the Harpos, when she showed up."

"I can't thank you enough for taking on this project," Artie said to Callie. "I'll finally be able to do a lot more than just sell leashes and Mutt Nuggets and aquarium stuff. I'll be able to take in a lot more rescue animals and help them

find homes. It's really a dream come true."

"You're lucky I love animals, too," Callie said. "It's why I'm giving you such a good deal. I'm not like those other contractors who are just out to fleece you."

Zeus's ears perked up. "Fleas? The human said 'fleas'! She wants the fleas, too?" He began sprinting in his exercise wheel again.

Zeus's outburst caught Callie's attention. "Hey, look at that cute little fella!" She pointed at the cage on the highest shelf above the counter.

"That would be Zeus," Artie said, "king of the critters."

"Zeus?"

"I name my favorite rescues after Greek gods."

"Huh. Maybe you should dress them in little togas and stuff," Callie mused. "That'd be adorable."

"Oh, I couldn't do that! Romans wore togas. Greeks wore chitons, which were like fancier togas."

"Uh, okay," Callie said. "Maybe dress them in those things then."

Artie laughed. "I love Greek mythology, but that seems a bit much."

Zeus looked down at his chiton and wondered not for the first time why humans never seemed to see it—or Athena's bracelets or Ares's helmet or any of the Olympians' enchanted attire. He supposed the humans just weren't worthy.

"Well, the Greek thing certainly explains the name of your place," Callie said, snapping Zeus back to their conversation.

"Let me give you the tour," said Artemis, waving toward the display shelves at the rear of the center. "Back there we have all our pet accessories: collars, scratching posts, cat beds, ball chuckers, that sort of thing."

"Selling accessories is what pays the bills, I bet," Callie said.

"It helps, although you'd be surprised how many kids want bugs." Artie pointed toward the glass case near the counter. Inside, Callie could see all manner of insects. "But I make every customer who buys a bug pledge they won't use it as bait."

"Okay, that's good, I guess." Callie sounded unsure.

"In the center of it all we have our fish tanks." Artie

waved an arm over the sea of aquariums in the middle of Mount Olympus Pet Center. "And here along the front window we have some of our star rescues."

"I take it this is one of them?" Callie handed her massive bag to Artie so she could pet the pug who was now drooling at her feet. "Who's a good pupper?"

"That's Ares, our resident god of war. Oof, what's in this thing?" Artie asked as she lugged Callie's bag to a nook by the aquarium tanks. She set it down and shook out her arm. "You pack the whole hardware store in here?"

"Oh, you know … just the basics. Tape measure, level, hammers, screwdriver … robot vacuum," Callie explained.

"Um, you threw a vacuum in your bag?" Artie asked in disbelief.

"Hey, jobs can get messy, and it's a super easy way to clean up," Callie responded. "Aww …" *Scritch, scritch, scritch.* She scratched Ares beneath his spiked collar. The little pug's lips pulled back in a slobbery grin. "He seems like a real sweetheart for a war god!"

"Don't get too attached," Artie said. "He's not up for adoption. I'd keep all my rescued animals if I could, but the ones I name after Greek gods are my personal pets."

"I suppose your favorite fish is named Poseidon?"

Artie laughed. "I think you and I are gonna have fun." She led Callie to the back of the shop, then paused beside a black crate on the floor.

"Hold on a sec," Artie said, "I better check on this guy." She kneeled down in front of the crate's metal door.

High on Mount Olympus, Demeter's eyes widened. "What's Artie doing at the cave down there?"

"I dunno. Artie stuff," Zeus said. "Who cares? I want to know where to find the Golden Fleas!"

Callie bent down next to Artie and eyed the crate. "That a new rescue?" Callie asked.

"Yep, just got him this morning. He'll stay in there until he acclimates to the place. I just want to see how's he's doing." Artie reached to open the crate's hatch.

"Artie, stop!" Demeter yelled. "There's a monster in there!"

Callie stood up. "You don't have a snake in there or something, do you? I'm not a fan of reptiles."

"Don't stress, Callie," Artie said, fumbling with the grate. "This little guy wouldn't hurt a fly—"

The hatch came open after a hard tug, sending Artie

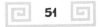

slipping onto to her backside. "Whoopsie!" She scrambled to secure it, but it was too late. A flash of something green and scaly darted out. It ran between Callie's legs—making her screech—before disappearing down an aisle.

Demeter couldn't believe her eyes. "Did ... did you see that thing, Zeus? Did you see what came out of the lair?"

Zeus shook his head. "All I saw was a green blur. Whatever it was ran thataway." He waved toward the Aegean Sea.

Artie stood up and brushed herself off. She looked around for the lost creature. "Well, I guess that's one way to acclimate him."

Callie stood frozen. "Was that a dragon? Because that looked like a dragon."

"A dragon!" Demeter repeated.

"A dragon?" Artie giggled. She put a hand on Callie's shoulder. "Trust me: That animal is more afraid of you than you are of him. We'll be fine. He'll be fine. He'll come out when he's hungry."

"When he's hungry?!" Demeter turned to Zeus. "Did you hear that, Zeus?! There's a hungry dragon on the loose!"

"Okay, if you say so." Callie shrugged. "Back to business, which I'm assuming is in here." She pointed to a nearby door with a handwritten sign taped to it:

Callie smirked. "No dragons either, I hope?"

Until this moment, as far as Zeus knew, that portal had always been closed and locked. Artie produced a key from her pocket. "Used to be a convenience store next door, but it's been vacant for months. The owner of the building agreed to rent it to me for cheap. Now I just need you to fix it up. Turn it into Mount Olympus two-point-oh." She opened the door and reached inside to flick on a light switch. "Welcome to uncharted territory, Callie."

Zeus's eyes went wide. "Uncharted territory …"

"Here there be monsters," Artie said.

Callie hesitated. "Monsters?"

"I mean not literally. But I do think we have a rodent infestation back here."

"Ah, well, I'll be on my guard." Callie giggled. She followed Artie into the vacant space next door. "Last thing you need in a construction zone are rogue rodents running willy-nilly ... So what do you have in mind for back here?" Their voices faded as the door fell closed behind them.

CHAPTER 6

UP ON MOUNT OLYMPUS, DEMETER BEGAN PACING IN FRONT OF ZEUS. Her words came out rapid-fire. "There's a hungry dragon on the loose. A. Hungry. Dragon. Just running free. I bet its belly is already starting to grumble. It won't go after Ares and Athena—they're too big. But everyone in the Bugcropolis is bite-size. We gotta stop that monster before it laps up my buddies like Mutt Nuggets!"

Zeus was staring through Demeter, not hearing a word. Hungry dragons weren't his priority right now. He had but one thing on his mind: the quest for the Golden Fleas, lost somewhere in uncharted territory. The Oracle's words kept running through his head: "You want your kingdom, you must find me the Golden Fleas."

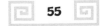

Zeus had to find them. They would prove to everyone—especially Poseidon—that he had what it took to rule Greece. He put his paws on Demeter's shoulders. "We have a new quest, buddy—the quest for the Golden Fleas!"

Demeter stepped back and crossed her four arms. "Uhhh, you mean *after* we stop the dragon, right?"

Zeus waved dismissively. "Yeah, yeah, dragon, whatever. It's not important. We need to find the fleas before that Callie lady does! She's probably digging around uncharted territory for them right now!"

"Let her! Who cares?!" Demeter shouted. She saw the cloud-shaped patch on Zeus's cheek quiver, a forecast of his foul mood. No one talked to the king of the Greek gods this way, except maybe Poseidon. Yet Demeter's friends were in danger.

"What's gotten into you?" Zeus asked.

"That dragon is getting ready to have a snack attack! And most of my buddies are bite-size. You want to know what's gotten into me—figure it out!"

"Sheesh, Demeter, calm down," Zeus said. "I'm sure your Bugcropolis friends can take care of themselves."

"You're just a morsel to that dragon, too, by the way!"

she snapped. "We need to assemble all the Olympians to come up with a strategy, and we need to do it *right now!*"

Zeus was as enraged as Demeter, but he didn't want to waste time arguing. "Fine," he replied. "Let's get the gang together." He poked his head through the columns of his palace and bellowed, "Olympians, assemble. Usual spot!"

The little hamster could be surprisingly loud when he wanted to. His voice reached every corner of Greece, and the lesser gods leapt into action. Athena popped up from her corner and stretched, her wiry orange mane poking everywhere with a serious case of cat-bed hair. Despite her bulky coat, she padded lightly over to the meeting place. One got the impression she was mostly fur.

Ares, by contrast, barreled past her like a bowling ball, barking, "Olympians assemble! Olympians assemble!" His helmet teetered wildly on the back of his head as he ran.

Zeus turned his attention to the Aegean Sea, scanning the surface for any sign of Poseidon. The pufferfish was the lord of the oceans, but Zeus was king of all the gods, and Poseidon dared not refuse his summons. At least Zeus hoped not. He was in no mood for the fish's attitude after Demeter's odd outburst.

Deep below the sea's surface, Poseidon lazily swam to a sea sponge near his coral throne and plucked out a trident, as much a symbol of his authority as the golden three-pronged crown on his head. Then he headed into a clear deep-sea diving helmet. It was large enough to fit Poseidon's spotted body and a supply of water once he sealed the faceplate. A long, skinny hose connected the helmet to a supply of oxygen-rich water that pumped over Poseidon's gills. The sea lord tapped his trident against the helmet, signaling a team of seahorses. Immediately they lifted the helmet to the water's surface, then lowered their lord down by the hose.

"Easy, lads!" Poseidon shouted. "Slow and steady!"

Once on solid ground, Poseidon swam against the side of his helmet, bumping into it over and over with his crowned head, scooching it in the direction of the meeting place. This portable fishbowl allowed the god of the Aegean Sea to travel in the realm of the air-breathing animals. In all his adventures on dry land, Poseidon had yet to reach the limits of his lifeline, the hose that snaked behind him and up to his ocean home.

Zeus had watched Poseidon emerge from his realm.

ART TO COME

Satisfied that the sea lord had answered his call, Zeus slipped through the hidden gate at the back of his palace and slid down the rope to the base of Mount Olympus, then looked up. "You coming, Demeter?!"

The cricket didn't answer. She just stepped to the edge of the palace and leapt toward the gathering spot, gliding to a soft landing on her retractable wings.

The Olympians always assembled at the Agora, an open area beneath Greece's northern cliffs surrounded by eight columns that were each wrapped in a coil of coarse rope.

"This had better not be a waste of my time, Zeus," Poseidon said testily. "I have my own kingdom to rule, you know." He tapped his three-pronged crown with his trident.

"Well," Zeus said in a measured tone, trying to avoid the old argument, "your kingdom is my kingdom, too, so—"

"It most certainly is not," Poseidon interrupted, puffing up slightly inside his helmet.

"It definitely is," Zeus said, anger creeping into his voice.

"Is not," Poseidon replied, puffing larger.

"Is, too!" Zeus countered. The cloud-shaped patch on

his cheek was quivering up a storm.

Athena stretched her two front legs against one of the rope-wrapped columns and began scratching at it. "Hey, you two, this is a really fascinating, helpful conversation, but I'm sure I don't need to remind you that Artie and her friend could walk back through that door at any moment, so, you know, we might want to move things along."

Zeus couldn't agree more. The sooner they got started, the sooner he would have those Golden Fleas, and the sooner he would show Poseidon who was boss. He looked around at the other Olympians and noticed someone was missing. "Hey, where's Ares … ?"

The pug trotted into the Agora, crumbs of Mutt Nuggets flying from his mouth.

Zeus gasped. "You took a detour to grab a snack?"

"Of course I did," Ares said. "You know I get fussy when I miss a meal." He plopped his meat-loaf-shaped body comfortably between Athena and Poseidon.

"You do get fussy," Athena agreed.

Tap. Tap. Tap. Zeus looked over to see Poseidon rapping his trident furiously against his dive helmet. "Oh, what now?" Zeus said.

"Why's Poseidon turning blue?" Demeter asked.

The pufferfish was pointing at the hose trailing from his helmet habitat, then to Ares. "Ares!" Athena leapt to her feet. "You're sitting on Poseidon's lifeline!"

"Yipe!" Ares hopped off.

Poseidon's healthy spotted coloring returned. "Watch where you put that muscle-bound behind of yours," he said weakly.

"Sorry 'bout that, Poseidon!" Ares said, his tail between his legs. Then he brightened. "Hey, but did you hear the good news? Zeus took care of that whirlpool monster for

ART TO COME

you."

"What whirlpool monster?" Poseidon asked.

Ares turned to Zeus. "You wanted us to tell him, right? The part about you sending that monster packing, not the part when Athena saved you from sleeping with the fishes."

"Which fishes?" Poseidon asked, looking lost. "Zeus, what's Ares going on about?"

Zeus puffed out his chest. "I vanquished Charybdis from your realm before he could swallow any more ships," Zeus answered. "And all without your help, Poseidon. You're welcome."

"You dared trespass in the Aegean Sea without calling on me first?!" Poseidon had puffed up again.

"Can it, fish!" Zeus said. "I'm calling on you now. I need everyone's help for this next quest." He looked nervously over his shoulder at the door to uncharted territory. "And we really do need to get moving before Artie and that other human come back."

"Ready when you are, boss," said Ares. "What's today's adventure?"

Zeus raised his paws dramatically. "It's a dangerous journey to a mysterious land for a powerful treasure.

Olympians, today we search for the Golden—"

"We're hunting a dragon!" Demeter had stepped in front of Zeus.

"A dragon?!" Athena, Ares, and Poseidon said at the same time.

"No, no, no, no!" Zeus said. "Not a dragon!"

"Where's a dragon?" Ares bowed, his helmet sliding into position over his face. "Where? Where?"

Demeter was taken aback. "Wait, am I the only one who knows about the dragon on the loose?"

"It's news to me," Athena said.

"Me, as well," Poseidon said.

"Seriously?" Demeter said. "None of you saw that scaly monster bolt toward the Aegean Sea?"

"Over there?" Ares sniffed in the direction of the Aegean. "Oooh, I'll find the dragon!" He ran off.

"No! Ares! Bad god! Bad!" Zeus jumped up and down, his voice growing hoarse. Poseidon's expression turned smug.

"Easy, Zeus," Athena said calmly. "Ares is just doing what he does. He is the god of war, after all. Just be glad I'm here doing what I do: keeping things on track. You were saying about our quest ..."

"Uh, right, thank you, Athena," Zeus said, regaining his composure. "We're after something much more important than any dragon."

Demeter started to speak, but Zeus planted a fuzzy paw over the cricket's tiny mouth, muffling any noises that tried to escape. "The Golden Fleas," Zeus said.

"That thing the Oracle was talking about?" asked Athena. "From 'Jason and the Argonauts'? The Golden Fleece?"

"Yeah, right, the Golden Fleas," Zeus said, releasing Demeter. "I'm pretty sure Callie's trying to find the fleas, too. So we need to get to them first."

ART TO COME

"Beg your pardon, King," Athena said, "but I believe you mean *fleece* not *fleas*."

Zeus scoffed. "I know what the Oracle said!"

"Why?" Poseidon asked.

"Why what?" asked Zeus.

"Why do we need to find this Golden Fleece?"

"Because I said so, that's why!" Zeus shouted. "Because I'm Zeus the Mighty, and leading you guys on adventures is what I do. I mean, am I crazy? Because I feel like I'm going crazy!"

Poseidon opened his mouth to reply.

"Don't answer!" Zeus cut him off. "That wasn't a serious question."

Poseidon twirled his trident and looked thoughtful. Finally, he said, "The Oracle told us Jason required a boat to find this treasure."

"Right!" Demeter perked up, sensing her chance to focus the other Olympians on her objective rather than Zeus's. "The *Argo*, a boat built by Athena." She turned to the cat. "You going to build us a boat, Athena?"

"Demeter, friend, this is the goddess of wisdom you're talking to." The cat cocked her head and grinned. "You need me to build a boat, I'm sure I could figure it out."

"Guys, c'mere!" It was Ares's voice from far away. The Olympians all looked around. "Over here!" Ares shouted. "I'm on Crete."

CHAPTER 7

CRETE WAS A STRIP OF LAND SURROUNDED ON THREE SIDES by towering dunes that held back the Aegean Sea. The Olympians arrived through the gap in the dunes that marked Crete's entrance to find Ares sniffing at what looked like a green mountain—at least it was the size of a mountain to the smaller Olympians.

"Did … did you find the dragon?" Demeter asked, looking everywhere at once.

"If he did, that's one funky-looking dragon," Zeus said. He joined Ares at the mountain, which was pitted with small caves. Zeus poked the side of it and felt it give slightly under his paw. Instead of rock, it was made of some sturdy fabric that seemed overstuffed, as if the mountain were about to burst. Zeus's expression changed from annoyance

to wonder. "Nice find, Ares," he said. "For once your complete lack of focus paid off."

"Thanks!" Aries nodded his helmet off his face and grinned a slobbery grin. He made a show of carefully checking for Poseidon's lifeline before plopping down and chewing on his foot.

Athena pawed at a label pinned high up on the side of the mountain. Printed on it were rows of small characters in a faded script:

Callista's Construction Company
If it ain't broke, I probably fixed it.
Athens, GA, 762-555-2368
Se habla español.

"What's it say?" asked Demeter.

"Perhaps it's a curse," suggested Athena.

"Maybe it says it's a vault full of Mutt Nuggets!" Ares said.

"It's definitely some sort of vault," Zeus said, "but it's not full of treats."

"It likely says 'Do Not Disturb,'" suggested Poseidon.

"Oh, you read Greek now?" Zeus scoffed. "I need a closer look up top. Athena, a boost?"

"Yeah, sure, I carry the collected wisdom of the ancients in my noggin and you want to use me as a stepladder." She lowered her head so Zeus, ignoring her gripes, could scramble upon her neck. He grabbed her ears above her golden laurel wreath as she stood on her hind legs and propped her front paws against the vault.

When Zeus was high enough, he leapt atop the vault. Everywhere he looked, intriguing objects were half-buried in or attached to the fabric surface. "Lot of cool relics up

ART TO COME

here, you guys!" He examined the closest object, a slim box made of a silver metal. "Hmm … " He tugged at it.

"Do not touch that!" Poseidon tapped his trident furiously. "It doesn't belong to you!"

The box didn't budge. Zeus probed behind it with his furry little fingers. He felt a metal clip on the relic's back, securing it somehow to the surface, so he tried sliding it instead of pulling it. The relic easily slipped free. "Got it!" Zeus said.

He began inspecting the artifact. It was bigger than his head but surprisingly light, with a small metal tab sticking from a corner. Zeus grabbed the tab and pulled. It was attached to the end of a rigid metal ribbon that unspooled from the box like a tongue. The ribbon was inscribed with skinny lines and large numbers that continued as Zeus revealed more of it. "Gosh, how long is this thing?" By the time he pulled the ribbon out to a line with the markings "1 Ft," its tip was touching the floor.

Athena batted her paw at the end of the ribbon, marveling at it. "How does such stiff metal fit in such a small box? This relic is surely enchanted."

"All the more reason to leave it be," Poseidon said.

Zeus went back to examining the silver metal box and noticed a small switch on the side of it. "What's this do?" He slid the switch.

THIIIPPPP!

"Hey!" Athena yelled. The ribbon had retracted suddenly—pulling her paw up along with it until she yanked it away.

"Do it again, Zeus!" she said.

"Don't encourage him," Poseidon replied. "That's not a toy."

"More like some kind of grappling hook," said Zeus. "I bet I could use this to climb up to all sorts of places!" He was delighted.

Poseidon was not. "Put it back!"

Zeus turned the boxy artifact in his paws. One side bore the image of a coiled snake. On the other side, Zeus found the metal clip that had held it to the vault. By slipping his fuzzy forearm through the clip, Zeus realized he could brandish it to protect himself.

"That grappling hook doubles as a shield!" Athena couldn't contain her enthusiasm. "It's like the aegis shield we heard about in the Oracle's tales, Zeus!"

"Oh, right, the aegis shield," Zeus said. "I knew that. This is the aegis, all right. Just look at how aegis-ish it is." Zeus quickly lifted his shield arm, which sent the aegis sliding off and tumbling over the side of the vault. "Look out below!" he shouted, but the silver shield had already hit the ground with a heavy thud.

"A little late," Demeter snapped. The shield had narrowly missed her head.

Zeus was already looking for more treasures. The vault's fabric felt firm beneath his feet. Whatever was crammed inside was hard and probably heavy. "We need to figure out how to open this thing, Olympians. Who knows what fabulous relics are hidden inside?!"

"What gives you the right to claim them?" Poseidon asked.

"Because they're here. Because I'm Zeus. And because I need them."

"We don't really have time to mess around with this," Demeter said. "I vote we leave it alone."

"It's a good thing this isn't up for a vote!" Zeus said, but then his expression softened as an idea struck him. "You know, Demeter," he said in a soothing tone, "I bet some of these doodads might come in handy if we want to stop your dragon."

Demeter gave Zeus a wary look. "Oh, so now you're suddenly open to the idea of stopping the dragon?"

"I'm *open* to being open about it." Zeus turned to Athena without waiting for a reply. "And, Athena, you're the second-wisest Olympian—after me, of course. Don't you want to see what other enchanted goodies are in this vault?"

She cocked her head. "It does pique my curiosity."

"Ares," Zeus continued, "uh, maybe there really are some Mutt Nuggets in this th—"

"I'm sold. Let's open it!" Ares replied immediately, his curly tail wagging in overdrive.

"Oh, wise up, everyone," Poseidon said. "Zeus is just trying to bribe you. Has anyone stopped to consider these artifacts might actually be dangerous?"

Zeus ignored him. He was rummaging again in the crannies. "Ho-ho! What have we here?" He had pulled out a black tube. It was skinny, lightweight, and a clear crystal was embedded on one end. Halfway down its side was a bump.

"Zeus, enough!" Poseidon shouted.

Ignoring the peeved pufferfish, Zeus peered into the relic's crystal tip. He reached his fingers down the metal tube and pressed the button.

"Gaaahhh!" A dazzling light erupted from the crystal an inch from Zeus's eyeballs. "I can't see! I can't see!" He dropped the tube and scrambled backward, paws over his eyes.

"Whoa, you okay, boss?" Ares asked, watching Zeus stumble above him. Everyone saw the beam shining from the other end of the tube as it rolled off the top of the vault.

ART TO COME

"It's like some kind of magic torch!" Athena said as the relic clattered at her paws. She jabbed at the button on its side and extinguished the light.

"Most likely it's one of Hekate's torches," Poseidon added. "Again: not a toy."

"Poseidon might be right," Athena added. "Hekate is the goddess of the dark arts: witchcraft and such. Perhaps we should leave it be."

"Nonsense," Zeus said, still stumbling around with his paws over his eyes. "What kind of dark art makes such a bright light?" He was backing blindly toward the edge.

"Watch your step, King!" Athena yelled.

"What?" Zeus felt his feet slipping. Frantically reaching for a handhold, he latched on to a stubby metal tab protruding from the fabric. "Whew," Zeus said, gripping the stub of metal with both paws. "I ... I think my eyesight's coming back. Just need to pull myself up—"

ZIPPPPPPP!

"No, no, no, no!" Zeus's weight was yanking the tab downward as he fell. The vault split open slowly in his wake. Large, heavy artifacts erupted from it, tumbling down the sides to the floor below. Some looked like beasts

with sharp teeth. Some looked like machines built for destruction.

"Avalanche!" cried Poseidon as he watched the titanic objects falling in his direction. "Look out, Olympians!"

CHAPTER 8

ZEUS SHUT HIS EYES. The farther he pulled the tab downward, the faster the vault spilled its contents. The Olympians scrambled to avoid the rain of objects. Demeter hopped away from a bulky contraption covered with coarse, papery skin. Poseidon's dive helmet took a glancing blow from a heavy red box, which then came to rest on his lifeline. Athena scurried out of the way of a tumbling machine that had a metal disc edged in jagged teeth. The artifact was so heavy its teeth lodged in the floor where it landed. Amid the chaos, Ares had stopped to scratch an itch under his collar with a hind leg. A black case landed on his helmet with a gonging

ART TO COME

kraaang and cracked open, spilling dozens of tiny, barrel-shaped objects that rolled in all directions across Crete. Ares sniffed at one of the shiny objects, shrugged, then went back to scratching.

Zeus felt his feet touching something hard. Opening his eyes, he saw he had ridden the tab safely down to the floor. The other Olympians were scattered among the relics before him. Everyone but Ares looked shell-shocked from dodging the avalanche. "Good news, everybody," he said cheerily. "Vault's open."

Above him, the vault entrance yawned like a cavern. The eruption of relics had slowed, but one last artifact tumbled out. It was the shape and size of Ares's food bowl, covered with mysterious switches and crystals. The artifact skidded down the side of the vault and landed on its edge, then teetered to fall flat on the floor with a loud thump. *BEEP-BOOP!* After a singsong series of beeps, the crystals around the edges of the round machine lit up as a motor inside it hummed to life. *WHIRRR!* The blue wheel-shaped relic began to glide along the floor, propelled smoothly by its hidden motor, hovering a half inch above the ground.

"Guys, what is that thing?" shouted Demeter, hopping

clear of the wheel's sudden charge.

It was barreling straight for Poseidon.

"Swim, Poseidon!" Zeus shouted beside the deflated vault in the center of Crete. "Swim for your life!"

Poseidon pressed against his mobile habitat and pumped his fins. The helmet didn't budge. His hose was still pinned beneath the red box that had nearly crushed him! Poseidon's lifeline was now a leash, and Poseidon was at the end of it. The pufferfish watched helplessly as the runaway machine bore down on him. "I … I seem to be in a spot of trouble here," he said, already sounding winded.

"God of war to the rescue!" Ares leapt between the machine and Poseidon's helmet at the last moment, forming a roadblock with his meaty body. The artifact rammed into the pug, paused, then rotated in place and bound away in a different direction at the same steady pace. "Hee!" Ares giggled. "That kinda tickled!"

"Well done, Ares!" Zeus yelled. "You scared it off!"

"I'm not out peril yet," Poseidon said weakly. "Might someone get this thing off my lifeline?" He pointed with his trident at the red box pinning his support line. "Someone with some muscles. It's frightfully heavy!"

"I got muscles!" Ares barked. He pressed his the brush-like plume of his helmet against the red box crushing the supply hose. "Nnnnng…" Ares pushed. "Nnnnng… Geez, this thing weighs a ton."

"Like I said … ," Poseidon gasped, "frightfully heavy."

The round machine whirred on. It bumped into one of the dunes at the borders of Crete, then immediately rebounded just as it had when it hit Ares.

"Watch out!" Athena swept Demeter aside moments before the machine could squash the cricket.

"I … I guess you didn't scare it off after all, Ares," Demeter said as Athena helped her to her feet.

"It almost seems … mindless," said Zeus, watching the contraption bounce off another dune.

"Whatever that thing is," Athena said, "it has an appetite. Keep an eye on those bits and bobs." She pointed to a few of the small shiny objects in the machine's path.

Everyone watched as the wheel rolled over the objects. *Clickety-clack! Clackety-click!* The machine rattled and rolled on. The metal objects were gone, sucked into its belly.

"Help me!" Ares shouted, panting hard. He had been slamming his body against the bulky red box pinning Poseidon's lifeline.

"I … I don't want to go to school yet, Mom," Poseidon mumbled. He looked deflated in his diving helmet, his crown about to slip off. "Just let me stay in bed for five more minutes."

"We're losing Poseidon!" Zeus raced to Ares's side and put all his weight against the red box. It didn't budge.

Meanwhile, the machine glided past Athena and Demeter and slammed into one of the heavy artifacts that had tumbled from the vault. Instead of bouncing off, the machine kept moving, pushing the object, shoving it against another dune. It then turned and glided off in a new direction.

Athena, watching all this unfold, said, "I have an idea."

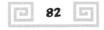

CHAPTER 9

ATHENA SPRANG ATOP THE MACHINE, which once again was bearing down on Poseidon's helmet. Her added weight didn't slow or alter its course, although its motor whirred a little louder.

"Isn't Atlantis just lovely this time of year?" Poseidon said dreamily. His skin was turning from spotty pale to a sickly blue again.

"Fish down!" Demeter shouted. "I repeat: Fish down!"

Athena sniffed at a cluster of symbols on the surface of the machine. The owl charm on her collar clanked softly against the machine's deck.

"Somebody … do … something," Zeus half said, half grunted, still pushing against the red box.

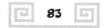

The machine was inches from smacking into Poseidon's helmet. Inside, the pufferfish was listing, going belly-up from lack of oxygen.

"Here goes … something!" The cat slapped a symbol with her paw. *Beep!* The machine abruptly changed direction, veering a hair's width to the left of Poseidon's helmet. Athena slapped another symbol. *Boop!* It turned right. Now it headed toward the red box that was crushing Poseidon's lifeline.

"I'm steering it!" Athena whooped.

ART TO COME

"You're about to crash!" Demeter shouted. "Hold tight, Athena!"

Athena sunk her claws into the rubber deck. *BOOM!* The machine smashed into the red box and kept rolling, pushing the box ahead of it.

Poseidon's lifeline was free and pumping oxygen-rich water into his helmet again.

"You … you did it!" cried Ares. The pug struggled to his feet and pressed his wet nose against Poseidon's helmet. "Breathe, buddy! Get some fresh air across those gills! Or fresh water! Or whatever!"

Poseidon's skin returned to its normal color. He sputtered, coughed, then swam right side up. "Wh-what happened?" he asked.

"You're not bound for the Underworld today, thanks to her." Ares nodded to Athena, who was still riding atop the machine.

She pawed at a large round button. *Beep, boop, boop!* The machine stopped in its tracks and went dark. "I figured out how to drive it, guys!" she said.

"Yay!" Demeter cheered.

"Woo-hoo!" shouted Ares.

"You saved Poseidon!" yelled Zeus.

"After you nearly killed me," Poseidon said, still catching his breath.

The Olympians cut off their celebration. "Uh, what?" Zeus asked.

"You unleashed that thing," Poseidon said matter-of-factly. "This is all your fault."

"My fault?" Zeus was flabbergasted. "I saved the day!"

"How?! By yelling at everyone else to do something?!" Poseidon began puffing up. "We wouldn't be in this predicament if you had just stayed away from the vault—like I told you to!"

The cloudy patch on Zeus's cheek quivered. "Nobody tells me what to do! I'm Zeus the Mighty!"

ART TO COME

Poseidon had puffed up so much that he was starting to squish against the sides of his helmet. His three-pronged crown looked tiny on his inflated head.

"Wow, Poseidon, you are really blowing up," said Ares, fascinated.

Athena had never seen Poseidon so angry. "Careful, sea lord!" she said. "You're puffed to capacity!"

"What makes you think you're worthy to rule anybody?!" Poseidon snapped at Zeus.

"Because … ," Zeus began, then faltered, "because I'm Zeus the Mighty!"

"Pffft." Bubbles streamed from Poseidon's mouth, and just like that, he deflated to normal size. "Well, I'm Poseidon the All-powerful!" He pointed a fin at Athena. "And that's Athena the Extraordinary!" He pointed to Ares. "And that's Ares the Stupendous!"

"Aww." Ares sunk to the floor. "Why do I have to be the stupid one?"

"No, no, 'stupendous,' not 'stupid,'" Poseidon corrected the pug. "You know what, never mind. You're just proving my point." He looked at Zeus. "Names are meaningless. It takes more than a name to prove yourself worthy to rule."

Zeus opened his mouth to reply but then closed it just as quickly. For the first time in his life, he didn't know what to say. He wanted those Golden Fleas more than ever. It was his big chance to prove to Poseidon he had what it took to claim all of Greece as his kingdom.

BOOP! Athena brought the machine back to life. She steered left, then right, then forward again. "I got this thing doing my bidding," she said, slapping the silver button that brought it to a halt. "I can drive it. It can take us places."

Zeus's eyes lit up. Once again, Athena was giving him the chance to put the quest back on track. "You can steer it, like, maybe … a vessel of some sort?" he suggested.

"Sure," Athena agreed.

"Perhaps a certain boat?" Zeus waved his paws encouragingly.

"Oh!" Athena exclaimed. "Like the *Argo*. This can be our *Argo*!"

"Bingo!" Zeus shouted. Poseidon rolled his eyes while Demeter slumped next to him.

"I mean," Zeus pressed on, "it makes sense. After all, according to the Oracle, it was Athena who built the *Argo* for Jason's quest. Now we have everything we need to find those Golden Fleas!!"

"Golden Fleas?" Ares tilted his head quizzically. "I thought we were going after a dragon."

"Fleece. The word is fleece," Athena corrected.

Zeus ignored Athena. "Ares, do try to keep up. Our next

big quest is to find the Golden Fleas, not chase after some make-believe reptile."

"Make-believe?" Demeter sounded hurt. "You told me you saw the dragon dart out of its lair! You told me you saw it run toward the Aegean Sea!"

"I said I saw a blur," Zeus corrected her. "It could've been a trick of the light."

"Um, Zeus?" Ares said, standing up.

"Or maybe you dreamed the dragon," Zeus pressed on. "You were pretty beat, Demeter."

"Zeus?" Ares said again, more urgently.

"We know the Golden Fleas are real." Zeus continued to ignore the pug. "The Oracle has spoken."

"Zeus, Zeus, Zeus!" Ares said.

"But no one else saw this dragon but you," Zeus said. "I'm sorry, Demeter, but I don't think it exists."

"ZEUS!" Ares shouted, spraying slobber.

"What?!" Zeus finally turned to Ares.

"You wanna tell *him* that he doesn't exist?" Ares pointed a paw at the entrance of Crete.

There, watching the Olympians through golden eyes, stood the massive dragon.

CHAPTER 10

THE DRAGON WAS LEAN AND LONG, at least as long as Athena. It hunched on four scaly legs that ended in cruel-looking claws. Its skin was greenish and banded with brown stripes. The scales around its jaws shimmered blue. Orange spines of leathery skin ran the length of its back. The dragon cocked its head to regard each Olympian in turn. Its tongue flicked out as if tasting the air.

"I *told* you there was a dragon!" Demeter shouted.

"I … I stand corrected," Zeus muttered, his eyes locked on the giant reptile. He backed away slowly until he bumped into the vault, then clutched at its loose fabric. The spiky fur on his head drooped over his crown.

"No sudden moves, anyone," Athena said, sinking low atop the *Argo* and arching her back.

"Why?" Ares asked. He had plopped down and was sniffing at his front paw.

"I don't know," Athena hissed. "It just seems like the right thing to say when you're facing a dragon." Athena's orange fur had poofed high in hackles.

The dragon remained motionless except for his eyes, which were sweeping from one Olympian to the next.

"Does this mean the quest for the fleas or whatever is on hold?" Ares stopped sniffing his paw.

"I should hope so!" Demeter said. "We have more important stuff to worry about! What if you-know-who here gets into the Bugcropolis? He'll gobble up my buddies!"

"Demeter makes a good point," replied Poseidon. "Reptiles and insects typically don't make the best of friends."

"Oh, so you're a dragon expert now?" Zeus shot back. "Maybe he'll just leave us alone." Zeus was not ready to abandon his quest.

The dragon took a step forward, then stopped, his tongue flicking, tasting the air.

"Reptiles and hamsters don't typically get along either," Poseidon added.

"I bet they get along better than hamsters and pufferfish," Zeus muttered.

"Guys," Athena said, "focus."

Demeter, meanwhile, had taken a few steps toward the vault. "You said I could use the stuff in the vault to stop the dragon, Zeus …"

The dragon cocked its head to follow her.

"Demeter," Athena whispered, "I don't want to scare

ART TO COME

you or anything, but the dragon seems to have taken an interest in you."

Demeter turned to look. Sure enough, the dragon was watching her intensely, its tongue flicking faster. It began lowering and lifting itself on its forelegs, as if doing push-ups. The spines on its back jiggled and flopped with each move.

"Ha!" Ares bowed on his front legs, then pushed up like the dragon. "I think the dragon wants to play!"

Demeter slowly backed closer to the vault. The dragon

ART TO COME

took a step forward. Its scaly belly and tail dragged on the ground, making a scraping sound. "No sudden moves, right?" Demeter asked.

"Hmm," Athena mused. "In your case, sudden moves might be good."

Demeter picked up her pace; the dragon matched it. "So much for the dragon just leaving us alone—oof!"

Demeter had tripped over Poseidon's lifeline and landed hard on her back. Before the other Olympians could react, the dragon charged.

It moved in a blur of orange spines and green scales and was just inches from the cricket, when something scooted into his path.

Poseidon's helmet. "Back, foul beast!" the pufferfish bellowed, brandishing his trident.

Demeter was struggling to get off her back, no easy task for a cricket.

The dragon butted its head against Poseidon's helmet, sending it skidding across Crete. Poseidon sloshed inside.

Nothing stood between Demeter and the dragon now. It opened its jaws and snaked out its tongue. The cricket closed her eyes.

ART TO COME

"Athena!" Zeus yelled. "Use the *Argo*!"

"Right!" she replied. *BEEP!*

Demeter felt the dragon's tongue flick across the lettuce sash on her chest. "Delicioussss!" the dragon rasped. Then ... nothing.

Slowly, Demeter opened her eyes. The dragon was gone. She heard the whirr of the *Argo* and saw Athena using it to shoo the monster away. The dragon eyed the *Argo* warily as it backed away, then looked back at Demeter. With one final flick of its tongue, the beast bolted through

the gap in the dunes that marked the gateway to Crete, disappearing onto the plains of Greece.

Zeus ran to Demeter and reached out a paw. She ignored him.

"Thanks, Athena!" Demeter cried instead. "The dragon obviously hates the *Argo*. You have to go chase off that beast before it attacks the Bugcropolis!"

"Oh, I am on it!" Athena said. *BEEP!* She guided the *Argo* to the exit of Crete, then stopped. "Zeus, I think we need to put the Fleece quest on pause. We have to save Demeter's friends!" She spurred the *Argo* back into motion and continued out of sight.

"Ooh, ooh, I want to play with the dragon, too!" Ares barked. "Wait for me, Athena!" The pug bounded past Zeus and Demeter and followed after the *Argo*.

Demeter finally took the outstretched paw of Zeus, who pulled his friend to her feet and dusted her off. "Look, uh, Demeter, buddy, I'm sorry ..."

"Save it," Demeter snapped, pushing Zeus's paws away. "I need to go make sure the Bugcropolis is safe."

Demeter's harsh words stung Zeus. "Don't worry, pal. The dragon will keep its distance," he replied.

"So now *you're* the dragon expert?" asked Poseidon, who had righted his helmet. "We all saw how that creature fixated on Demeter. It clearly has a taste for cricket."

Demeter winced. "I … I gotta go." She launched herself through a gap in the dunes and off of Crete.

Zeus stood alone with Poseidon. The pufferfish made a dramatic show of peering in every direction, then eyed Zeus smugly. "Looks like 'Zeus the Mighty' is ruling a pretty small kingdom these days."

Zeus stayed silent. He was too upset to argue.

"I knew it would take more than a name to inspire loyalty in your minions." The pufferfish spun in his helmet and started scooching in the same direction Demeter had headed. "I'd love to stay and gloat, but I have *actual* loyal subjects to rule."

Zeus watched Poseidon leave, then turned to look up at the empty mountain of fabric in the middle of Crete. He felt strangely empty himself. The Zeus according to the Oracle's weekly tales was all-powerful, the king of the gods. He brought order and law to Greece. But Zeus didn't feel that way right now. The Olympians had defied him. Abandoned him.

He had focused only on the fleas, and now Demeter and her friends were in danger.

Zeus's spiky hair drooped nearly into his eyes. He was wandering aimlessly when his toe struck something hard beside the vault. "Oww! What the … ?" He looked down and saw the first relic he'd discovered, the aegis with the rigid ribbon inside. He picked up the slim metal box and turned it over to find the clip on its back. Slipping his forearm though the clip, he wielded the silver shield. "I need all the protection I can get," Zeus mused. Then he spotted the tube-shaped torch—one of the goddess Hekate's torches, claimed Poseidon, that pompous pufferfish. The torch had blinded him, but now he knew how it worked. Doubtless it would come in handy. "Better take that, too."

Loaded up with relics, Zeus followed where the other Olympians had gone, to the gap in the dunes that marked the exit of Crete. He had come to this place sure of who he was, surrounded by faithful followers, and ready for the quest to find the Golden Fleas. Now he was alone and full of doubt. "Well, at least things can't get any worse," he mumbled.

ART TO COME

And that's when Zeus tripped over a giant shoe. It belonged to Artie, who was standing just outside Crete with Callie.

They had returned from uncharted territory.

CHAPTER 11

"**A**RE YOU GETTING THIS?**" Callie giggled. "Please tell me you're getting this!"

"Ha! Oh, yeah!" Artie could barely control her laughter. "This'll be viral gold! The best advertising for the store!"

"The best," Callie agreed.

Zeus couldn't see what the two were talking about. As soon as he stumbled over Artie's foot, he scrambled back to Crete and dove into the vault, cowering in its loose fabric. Somehow he had managed to keep hold of the aegis shield and the black torch. The bigger miracle was that Artie and Callie hadn't noticed him. The two had returned from the portal next door quietly, but now they were laughing loud enough to raise the dead from the

ART TO COME

Underworld. Zeus wanted to see why.

He set the two relics down and poked his head out of the vault. Artie and Callie were standing just off of Crete, watching something on the plains of Greece. Artie was holding the black rectangle from which the Oracle told its tales. She was holding it in front of her, almost as if she were showing it something.

"Ooh, zoom in. Get closer," Callie said. "Your kitty is making the funniest expression!" Artie and Callie walked slowly out of sight of Zeus.

He had to see what all the fuss was about. He hopped out of the vault and scampered after the two humans. He could still hear them giggling and … something else. It sounded like a faint whirring noise. A familiar sound. The *Argo*! Zeus scurried silently to the edge of Crete and peeked out at the plains of Greece. The first thing he noticed was Ares, nearby in his messy chambers. "Pssst!" Zeus hissed. "Why didn't you warn me that Artie and her friend were back?"

Ares said nothing. Zeus couldn't tell if he was ignoring him or just distracted. Something high above Zeus held the pug's attention. Zeus saw Callie and Artie with their backs to him. So he sprinted across the plain to the front of Ares's home.

"Oh, hey," Ares said through a mouthful of Mutt Nuggets. His bronze helmet was propped so far back on his head that its plume brushed the ceiling of his chambers. "Isn't this exciting?"

"Isn't what exciting?" Zeus clutched the columns while he caught his breath.

"Poseidon's happy homecoming," said Ares. He pointed a paw up toward the Aegean Sea while popping bits of Mutt Nuggets in his mouth.

"Poseidon?!" Zeus looked. The pufferfish was still in his diving helmet, which was suspended from its lifeline about two feet below the edge of the Aegean Sea. A team of seahorses pulled the helmet upward little by little, hoisting their king up the cliff face to his aquatic realm. Brandishing his trident, Poseidon urged his minions on. "Haul away, boys! Haul, I say!" he ordered. The seahorses heaved and the helmet lifted again.

"What's that fool doing?" Zeus said. "Artie will catch him!" But Artie and Callie weren't paying any attention to Poseidon. Instead, they were focused on Athena, who was

driving the *Argo* in circle so tight she was nearly spinning in place.

"Don't hurl up a hairball, Athena," said Artie, who had knelt to hold her device at a different angle.

"I've seen online videos of cats riding robot vacuums before," Callie said, "but never like this. It almost looks like your kitty is *driving* that thing."

Zeus turned back to Ares, his eyes going wide. "Is Athena putting on a show to give Poseidon time to get home?"

"Yep," said Ares. "It was quick thinking on her part. Artie and Callie just kinda snuck up on everyone from uncharted territory. I was lucky I had gone home for a snack."

"That's not really luck. When do you ever skip a snack?" Zeus was struck by a sudden thought. "Hey, where's Demeter?"

Ares shrugged. "Last I saw her she was chasing that dragon toward the Bugcropolis, with Athena in hot pursuit. Then Artie and Callie came back, and, well, here we are."

Zeus peered way up at his palace atop Mount Olympus, hoping to see Demeter lounging against the columns.

He immediately felt foolish. Demeter wouldn't have run home, not with that dragon still on the loose.

He felt sick.

"Looks like Athena's game is over," Ares said, snapping Zeus back to the situation at hand. Artie had scooped Athena off the *Argo*. The machine glided away without her. "What's the plan, boss?"

Zeus glanced back at the Aegean in time to see Poseidon's helmet safe back in the water. The pufferfish popped open the faceplate and swam into open water, stretching his fins. He stuck his trident into the sponge on the seafloor and came to rest on his seat of coral next to it—his throne—while a team of colorful shrimp cleaned and stowed his diving helmet.

Zeus considered his next move. If he helped Demeter, Callie or someone else might find the fleas before him. But if he chased the fleas, Demeter would never forgive him. Worse, she might fall prey

ART TO COME

to the dragon!

Zeus sighed. "I guess the quest for the Golden Fleas will have to wait," he told Ares. "Demeter and her friends can't. As long as that dragon's on the loose, they're in danger."

"We're gonna go stop the dragon?!" Ares yipped. "Oh boy, count me in—"

"Shhh!" Zeus stuck his paw into Ares's chamber and clamped the pug's lips shut. "Eww!" He quickly pulled it away and shook off globs of slobber.

"Okay, Athena, I think you've had enough fast and furious racing for one night," Artie was saying.

"More like the fast and the furriness," Callie said, giggling. "That's what you should call the video when you post it. Although knowing you, you'll just name it after something from ancient Greece."

"Maybe 'Athena and the *Argo*.'"

"Hey, I like that." Callie tapped the big round button on the *Argo*'s deck with her shoe. "Time to drop anchor, *Argo*," she said. "Now if we can just get some of these other critters to join Athena's crew, they can be her Argonauts."

Zeus white patch twitched. "Whatever," he muttered.

He should be the captain of the Argonauts, not Athena!

"I've never seen a robot vacuum quite like that one," Artie said, cradling Athena and petting her head.

Callie picked up the *Argo* and gave it a shake. It made a rattling sound. "Yeah, it's a heavy-duty model. More like a shop vacuum." She inspected the display on its top. "I was hoping to cut it loose next door tonight, but it looks like it needs recharging. Where did you put my duffel again?"

"Over here," Artie said, leading Callie back toward Crete.

"They're heading this way, boss!" Ares shouted. "Run!"

Zeus didn't need to be told twice.

CHAPTER 12

EUS SCRAMBLED BACK IN THE DIRECTION OF NEARBY CRETE, away from Callie and Artie. He was nearly to the gap in the dunes marking the entrance to the island, when he chanced a peek over his shoulder. "Oww!" Zeus tripped on one of the shiny bits that had fallen from the vault and fell to the ground.

"Hey, hey," Callie said. "Looks like you have another Greek god on the loose."

Zeus froze. He couldn't see Callie, but she sounded close, with Artie was right behind her. Slowly he rolled onto his back, expecting to find them standing over him.

But their attention was focused on Ares, who was out of his chambers and chasing his stubby tail. Ares paused to glance at Zeus and just barely nodded his head toward

Crete. He was urging Zeus to flee.

Zeus bolted for the entrance to Crete. Once on the island, he leapt into the vault to hide.

"Yep, that's my god of war," Artie said, scooting Ares back into his palace. "Always up to no good." She turned to Callie. "I swear, normally this place isn't such a zoo."

"If you say so," Callie said as she squeezed into the nook between the aquarium cases and spotted the avalanche of items that had spilled from the vault. "Looks like Athena got a lot more than the vacuum out of my bag."

"Oh, gosh, sorry, Callie," Artie said, stepping up behind her.

"Sockets everywhere. Now I know what's rattling around inside the vacuum. No big deal." She began tossing the shiny barrel-shaped objects back into her bag.

"Oww!" Zeus ducked as metal objects began raining down around him inside the vault. Then Callie started cramming in larger tools, and the hamster scurried deeper into the vault.

"Power sander looks okay." Callie ran her hand along the tool's belt of rough sandpaper before stuffing it away. "Yikes! My buzz saw." She tugged at the tool at her feet. Its

blade was stuck in the floor.

"Uh-oh," Artie said. "You cut yourself?"

"No, no. The saw's blade is stuck in your floor. Athena's lucky she didn't get cut—curiosity might've killed the cat." Callie gave a yank, and the circular blade pulled free. She placed it carefully in the bag, which was once again stuffed to near bursting. "Everything accounted for?" Artie asked.

"Yeah, this time," Callie said. "I think I better move this stuff way out of range of your nosy cat."

In the black depths of the vault, the heavy artifacts around Zeus began to tilt and tumble. He was fighting to keep his balance, when something hard conked him on the head. The little hamster felt himself falling into nothingness.

CHAPTER 13

ZEUS THE MIGHTY WOKE WITH A BLINDING HEADACHE. Or was he really blind? Zeus was pretty sure his eyes were open, but he couldn't see a thing.

In his panic over his lost eyesight, he sat up too quickly. "Nnnnngh." A mistake. His head ached! Actually, it wasn't so much a headache as a head *quake*. It felt like Poseidon was banging his trident inside his noggin.

Thinking of Poseidon brought back other memories. Athena driving the *Argo* in circles to distract Artie and Callie. The dragon chasing after Demeter. *Demeter!* It all came flooding back. Demeter had run off to protect her friends from the dragon, and Zeus hadn't gone with her.

Now he was lost in the darkness, unable to help his best

friend.

Zeus realized his heart hurt worse than his head. And he still couldn't see. Another memory clicked into place. *I'm still in the vault of enchanted relics!*

Speaking of relics ... Zeus fumbled around the bottom of the vault until his paw brushed a familiar tube-shaped object. He reached for its button.

Click.

At first, the light from Hekate's magic torch was as blinding as the darkness, but as his eyes adjusted, Zeus picked out familiar shapes: bulky machines, sharp edges,

ART TO COME

the aegis shield that had started all his problems. He scooped it up and began picking his way up the pile of artifacts, using them as steps. He knew the only way out was up, but as Zeus clambered higher, the space around him grew tighter. The heavy artifacts pressed against the fabric of the vault, blocking the exit, which was sealed as well.

Zeus was trapped.

"There's gotta be a way out of here." He swung his torch around the cramped space. "Oww!" His paw had brushed against something sharp: a large machine with a metal disc edged with jagged teeth. Zeus carefully ran his fingers across the teeth. The disc rotated when he touched it. This gave him an idea.

He started twisting and shoving the artifact. "Just one more push," Zeus said, grunting. "There!" Now the toothy machine lay on its side, with its jagged teeth pressed against the fabric of the vault's wall. Zeus wedged the light into a cranny so he wouldn't have to hold it, then slowly climbed onto the disc, careful not to touch the pointy edges himself. "Well," Zeus said to himself, "here's where all that time on the ol' exercise wheel pays off."

Zeus put one foot forward, then another. His steps forced the disc into motion. Zeus worked up to a trot, spinning the disc faster. The trot became a jog, then a brisk run, then a full sprint. The sharp teeth scraped against the side of the vault.

"I … hope … the wall of this vault … wears out before I do," Zeus panted. He silently vowed to spend more time in his wheel.

A tear appeared, and quickly grew into a gash as big as the blade itself. "That … that should do it," Zeus said, and slowed to a stop. He grabbed Hekate's torch and poked his head through the hole he had cut in the vault.

The world outside was as black as it had been inside, so Zeus retrieved the magic torch and aimed it through the gash. Wherever he was, it was a vast space. The air was hot and still. "I don't think I'm in Greece anymore."

CHAPTER 14

THE PLACE LOOKED LIKE A DARKER, DIRTIER, DESERTED VERSION OF GREECE. Similar to Zeus's realm, it sprawled with mountains and valleys and towering structures, barely visible in the dim torchlight. But whereas Artie tended to Greece's landscape, tidying and supplying it, this land felt abandoned, lifeless. Cliffs and mesas, empty except for a few colorful crates of what looked like human food, loomed out of the gloom. Specks of dust hung in the torchlight. Zeus wondered if there was a sea like Greece. He sniffed at the still air but detected no fresh salty smell. Instead, it stank of musty old scrolls and rot.

That's when he realized: "I'm in uncharted territory!

Callie must have dragged the vault in here!"

Zeus felt a thrill. If he was in uncharted territory, perhaps the Golden Fleas were close! And since he was already here, he might as well grab them. Just thinking about the fleas made Zeus's white patch itch. He began panning the torch around eagerly, hoping for a glint of gold or … any sign of the fleas. Shadows danced wildly.

"Hey!" a distant voice yelled from deeper in the room. "Who summoned the sunrise?!"

Zeus squeaked and switched off the torch. Uncharted territory was once again plunged into darkness.

"I know someone's there," the voice called. "No use hiding! Come out! Show yourself!"

Zeus considered keeping quiet. Maybe whoever was out there would just give up and go away. But then again, he was Zeus the Mighty. The king of the gods didn't cower in the dark. Plus, he was curious. "Who are you?" he bellowed.

"I asked you first," the voice shot back.

Zeus sighed. He switched the torch on again and shined it into the void. Nothing. "Stay where you are," Zeus yelled. "I'll come down and introduce myself."

"Fine," the voice replied. "Just don't expect me to share my supper. I barely get enough to eat as it is."

Zeus dug around the bottom of the vault for the aegis shield, then shoved it through the rip in the fabric and let it fall to the floor. He squeezed through the rip carrying Hekate's torch. He slid down the outside of the vault and landed nimbly. He found the aegis and slipped it over his forearm, tucked the torch under his arm, and set off in the direction of the voice.

CHAPTER 15

ZEUS FOCUSED ON THE BEAM LIGHTING HIS
PATH. Peering off to the sides—and into the pitch
blackness—made him uneasy. Cliffs and hillsides
loomed into view, then faded behind him. The silence
wasn't helping, so Zeus decided to strike up a conversation
with the mystery voice. "So, uh, what's for supper?" Silence.
"Um, hello?" Zeus tried again. "Mr. Mystery Voice? I can't
very well introduce myself if you don't speak up. How will
I find you?"

"Shh! Quiet!" The voice sounded close.

"What's the proble—"

"Shush up!" the voice cut him off. "They'll hear you!"

A chill ran up Zeus's spine. "Who'll hear me?" He cast

the light around. It illuminated a wall, and a boxy metal structure next to a tall portal. But not the owner of the mystery voice.

"Will you shush?!" The voice sounded panicked. And closer than ever.

All was quiet, and then: faint flapping. "Oh gods, here they come!" the voice squeaked.

SCREEE!

The noise, like claws down a windowpane, froze Zeus's blood. It came from above. He tilted the torch up toward the sound—then nearly dropped it out of terror. "Gaaahhh!" Zeus screamed.

The creature was black, with a furry body larger than his. It had leathery wings stretched between spindly fingers, which were tipped with nails that looked as sharp as the claws on its fuzzy feet.

"What in blazes is that?!" Zeus shouted. No sooner had that monster darted away from his light than another swooped down from the darkness, clawing at Zeus's head. He barely had time to raise his shield.

"How many of those things are there?" Zeus yelled. He had dropped to a knee and was panning his torch around.

"It depends," the mystery voice answered. "Sometimes it's just a few. Sometimes I swear it's the whole colony."

"Whole colony!" The storm-cloud patch on Zeus's cheek shook.

"It's best if you just ignore them and let them do their own thing." The voice sounded strangely calm. "Hamster meat isn't really on their menu, but if you put up a fight, they will fight back. Trust me."

"Hamster meat?" Zeus was taken aback. "How'd you know I'm hamster?"

"I wasn't talking about you," the voice said.

Zeus was trying to make sense of this response when a blur of motion at the fringes

ART TO COME

of his torchlight caught his eye. He shifted it in time to catch two creatures diving right for him. The little hamster closed his eyes tight and hugged his torch. The winged monsters flew directly into the beam and began screeching and darting out of the light. Finally, everything went quiet and Zeus slowly opened one eye. "Whatever they are, they don't like the light," Zeus said.

"We don't get much light around these parts."

Zeus knew he had to shine the light up to ward off the attacking creatures, yet curiosity was eating at him. Who was the source of the mystery voice? Deciding to chance it, he swung the beam in the voice's direction—and was shocked to see a hamster dressed in a ripped, ragged cloak hunkered on the ground with his arms wrapped around his head. Zeus couldn't see his face, but his body was thin and frail-looking beneath his rags. His fur was gray from head to toe.

Scattered around the hamster were what looked like crumbs of food. As Zeus watched, more crumbs tumbled from above. "Where … where'd all the food come from?"

"From the creatures," replied the cowering hamster. "They drop lots of crumbs when they raid the crates for

treats. I call dibs on all these morsels—that is, if they leave me any, which they usually don't."

Zeus heard flapping and shifted the light to see one of the creatures reach with its talons for some fruit-shaped treats that had spilled from a colorful crate on a nearby cliff. When the beam hit it, the creature screeched and flew away empty-handed. Zeus whirled the light and saw creatures everywhere, too many to count, all clawing at the scraps on the cliffs and the ground.

"They're running out of treats up top," said the old hamster, sounding defeated. "Now they're here for the leftovers. Guess I'm going hungry for another day. Story of my life."

Zeus kept the light moving to ward off the creatures, when he remembered the final words of the Oracle's tale. "Phineus!" Zeus hissed.

"Huh?" said the cowering hamster.

"You're Phineus, the blind soothsayer! And these are the Harpies always snatching your food!"

"Well, yeah, that's pretty much what they do, day in and day out. Not that I can really tell one day from the next here."

"You can see the future! You can help me stop the dragon! You can help me find the Golden Fleas!" Zeus was overjoyed.

"You get me something to eat and I'll help you land on the moon if you want," the gray hamster shot back.

The Harpies' screeching grew more frantic. They were still hungry. Zeus heard wings flapping behind him just in time to spin and raise his shield. Sharp claws raked across it. The air hummed with the beat of Harpy wings. "This torch isn't cutting it," Zeus said. "When's the blasted sun come up around here?"

"Oh, about never o'clock, unless you count the magical kind of sunlight, but even that's rare."

Zeus had seen Artie conjure light—usually with the flick of her finger near portals. He understood what the hamster was talking about. He recalled noticing a portal while trekking across uncharted territory.

Zeus took off, leaving the old hamster cowering in the darkness.

"You're running away?" the gray hamster cried. "Coward!"

But Zeus had a plan.

CHAPTER 16

ZEUS THE MIGHTY SPRINTED ACROSS UNCHARTED TERRITORY. The shield and torch relics felt like anchors in his arms; he'd drop them if they weren't essential to his survival.

"Where is the blasted portal?" he muttered, panting. The torch bounced as he ran, making it hard to focus on the path in front of him. He should have reached it by now. Had he gone in the wrong direction? "Why does uncharted territory have to be so … uncharted?"

He heard the familiar beating of wings behind him. "Harpies!" Zeus squeaked. He dove and rolled, then hopped to his feet in time to see one of the creatures gliding away in front of him. "Ha! Missed me!"

Zeus shifted his grip on the torch and continued his sprint—but his evasive move had taken a toll. His legs ached. His lungs burned. His vision blurred. He was about to collapse from exhaustion, when the portal he remembered finally loomed in front of him. "Oh … thank gods."

Zeus skidded to a halt and leaned over with his paws on his knees, fighting to catch his breath. A strip of familiar red light radiated below it. "It's … it's the portal back to Greece!"

Harpy screams rang out around him, snapping Zeus into action. The creatures were clearly angry that he had interfered with their dinner. He whipped the torch around to keep them at bay, and his light fell upon precisely what he was looking for. High up the wall next to the portal sat the object he had seen Artie use so many times. "Bingo."

Zeus examined the large metal box against the wall near the portal. He could make out seams in the metal, probably panels for accessing the box's contents. "Another vault full of magical relics, no doubt," Zeus muttered, but he wasn't interested in what was inside this vault.

He needed to get on top of it.

Zeus slipped the aegis off of his forearm. "Time to see if this thing really works."

Zeus stood. Hekate's torch on its end, creating a cone of light the Harpies dared not enter. He then positioned the aegis on the floor and pulled on the tab at its side. Out came the rigid metal ribbon inscribed with those same skinny lines and symbols. By the time "4 Ft" slid into view, the ribbon's tip was nearly level with the top of the metal vault. "Almost there," Zeus said, squinting up into the gloom. "One more pull."

Clunk!

Zeus whooped. The tip had latched on to the top of the vault. Zeus tugged on the ribbon, but it held firm. "Ready for liftoff!" Zeus sat atop the shield with his back to the ribbon. He tucked the torch under his arm, keeping its beam pointed up to ward off the Harpies. With his free paw, he reached for the switch on the shield's side. "Going up!" Zeus braced himself and slid the switch.

Nothing happened. "Uh-oh," Zeus said. He gave a solid kick to the aegis beneath him and it lurched upward. "Okay, here we go!" Zeus felt the ribbon sliding along his back as

ART TO COME

the shield box carried him up. But it moved much slower than he expected and soon came to a halt. Zeus pointed the light down and saw he was only a foot above the floor of uncharted territory. "C'mon!" Zeus shouted, banging the relic and swinging his legs. "Giddy-up!" The aegis swayed but didn't budge.

A flash of leathery wings caught Zeus's eye. He moved his light just in time to blind a Harpy, which screeched and darted away. Dangling midair on the thin ribbon, he must have looked like bait at the end of a hook to the creatures.

Zeus swung the torch wildly. It began to feel heavy under his arm. Very heavy ... "That's it!" Zeus exclaimed. "I'm too heavy!" If he wanted to make the trip up, he'd have to lighten his load. That left Zeus with only one option.

He would have to drop the torch.

He'd have no way to repel the Harpies. He'd be blundering about in total darkness to complete a task he wasn't even sure would work. Zeus pondered reversing the switch and sliding back to the floor, but then he would be trapped in uncharted territory. Another Harpy barreled out of the blackness. Zeus blinded it but not before it lashed out and nearly knocked the torch from his arm.

"Enough's enough!" he yelled.

He dropped the torch.

ZIIIPPPPPP!

The shield launched upward, nearly tumbling Zeus from his seat. He squeezed his legs tight to hold on. Below, the flashlight clattered to the floor and went off, casting uncharted territory back into blackness.

CHAPTER 17

ZEUS'S RAPID ASCENT ENDED SO ABRUPTLY, he was thrown off the shield and landed on the edge of the metal vault's top, his feet dangling off of it.

Bang! Something large and heavy slammed into the vault door below him. Zeus could see nothing, but he knew one of the Harpies had swooped for him and missed. "Ha!" he yelled. "Too slow!"

Furious screeches erupted around him, and Zeus immediately regretted his taunt. The darkness was thick with Harpies.

Zeus scrambled away from the edge and inched in the direction of what he hoped was the wall, holding his paws in front of him. His fuzzy little fingers were now his eyes.

He wiggled them, expecting to brush the wall at any moment.

Where was the wall? A horrible thought struck him. What if he'd gotten turned around in the dark? Was he about to tumble over the edge?

Thump.

Zeus flinched. Something heavy landed next to him.

Thump. Thump. Thump. Zeus realized that although he was blind, the Harpies could probably see just fine. And now they were landing all around him. The storm cloud on his cheek quivered.

Thump. Thump.

The screeching had stopped, but Zeus could hear ragged breathing … and a new sound: soft squeaks, at the limits of Zeus's hearing, but terrifyingly close.

Something brushed against his fingertips. "AAAHHH!" he screamed. Then he realized what he felt was the wall. "Yes!" He pawed frantically for what he knew was there.

Squeaking now surrounded him. "Come on, where is it?" His fingers found a bump in the wall. He slid his paw left and right, up and down, searching for a shape poking from the wall. The squeaks were now rapid-fire, almost

like clicks. "It's gotta be here," Zeus hissed.

The spiky fur on his head stirred, as if ruffled by a hot breeze. No, not a breeze. It was hot, gasping breath.

Finally Zeus found what he'd been looking for, the stubby object he had seen Artie flip to summon light. His paws closed around it. The clicks were constant now, almost deafening. "Let there be light!" he shouted, and wrenched the object upward.

Pitch black became pure white.

The air filled with furious screeches.

Zeus's eyes were dazzled by the sudden light, and he looked down to block the glare. As his vision adjusted, he noticed clawed feet surrounding him. Zeus looked up to see at least two dozen Harpies encircling him, each wrapped in its black wings to block out the harsh light.

Zeus pushed his way through the thicket of huddled Harpies. "Coming through. Pardon me. Beg your pardon." He treaded carefully to avoid stepping on their clawed feet. But just as he made it to the last row, his foot came down on a talon. "Ooh—sorry!"

SCREEEEEEEEE!

The creature unfolded its wings and launched into the

ART TO COME

air. In a chorus of hideous screams, the entire colony exploded into flight, buffeting Zeus with their wings. He watched the Harpy cloud race across uncharted territory and squeeze into a cave on a distant mountain.

CHAPTER 18

ZEUS THE MIGHTY GAZED OUT ACROSS UNCHARTED TERRITORY. The cliffs and mountains he had passed in darkness looked much larger in the light he had summoned. They were arrayed in rows across the whole space. Most were barren. Atop a few sat colorful crates, some of which were ripped open with crumbs scattered around.

He also spotted the gray hamster writhing on the ground with his paws pressed over his eyes. "Phineus!" Zeus called. He had forgotten all about the soothsayer he'd left cowering in the dark. "Hang tight!" Zeus shouted. "I'll be right down."

"Where do you think I'm gonna go?" Phineus replied.

"Miami?"

Zeus prepared to ride the aegis back to the floor, when a thought occurred to him. He grabbed the shield and moved to the ledge nearest the portal. Peering down, he spotted the knobby object he was looking for. It was halfway between him and the floor. Zeus figured he might be able to reach it if he planned his descent just right. He carefully reattached the aegis's tab to the ledge, hopped aboard, and released the relic's switch.

ZIIIPPP! Zeus kept his eyes on the knobby object in the portal as he dropped. He was falling fast. Zeus had seen Artie open all sorts of portals. He knew he would only get one chance. He kicked at the object as he dropped past it. He didn't see anything happen but heard a low click. The effort had thrown Zeus off balance, and he barely managed to stay aboard the shield until it hit the floor, where he tumbled in a heap.

"Well, that wasn't fun," Zeus said, brushing himself off. He hadn't opened the portal as he'd hoped. The doorway to Greece seemed the barest bit ajar, but it was much too heavy for him to move.

Zeus felt homesick. And helpless. He couldn't even see

the familiar glow of Greece under the door now that the lights were on. He knew Demeter and her Bugcropolis friends might be fending off the dragon on the other side of the portal, and he could do nothing.

"I guess this is my life now," Zeus said, looking around uncharted territory. "I might as well make the most of it." He yanked the aegis free from the metal vault and retracted its ribbon, then slid it onto his forearm. He located his torch, confirmed it still worked, and set off in the direction of Phineus.

The soothsayer remained where Zeus had left him. Zeus was struck by just how ancient he looked. His whiskers had grown nearly to his waist, forming a sort of stringy beard. He looked weak and confused as he blinked against the light.

"You all right, old-timer?" Zeus asked.

"I've been better," Phineus said as he stood up cautiously and produced a slim cane, which he leaned on. "I've been worse, too, I guess. At least I can see again—" Phineus cut himself short as his gaze fell upon Zeus. His beady eyes went wide. "You're … you're Zeus!"

"Yep," Zeus said.

"Zeus the Mighty!"

"Uh-huh, that's me," Zeus confirmed. "I'd heard you soothsayers are real know-it-alls."

"Oh, uh, yeah," Phineus said, "we say the sooth, the whole sooth, and nothing but the sooth. That's what soothsayers do. Heh." He looked toward the portal to Greece. "Artie still playing those tales about heroes and monsters and such out there?"

"The Oracle? Yeah! *Greeking Out* is my favorite!"

"Of course it is." Phineus smiled an odd little smile and winked. He spotted a brown crumb on the floor and stuck it with his cane, brought it to his mouth, then nibbled at it.

Zeus's belly let out an alarmingly loud grumble. "Ho, ho!" Phineus said. "Somebody skipped breakfast. When's the last time you ate, son?"

"Umm … I don't remember," Zeus said. "A lot's happened lately." Pangs of hunger clawed at his stomach, which unleashed another loud growl.

Phineus looked at the crumb on the tip of his cane, then looked at Zeus, then back at the crumb. His shoulders slumped and he sighed loudly. "I guess I owe you one, son." He held the crumb up to Zeus's face. "Chow down." Without hesitation, Zeus snatched the crumb and began devouring it. Phineus said, "Least I can do is feed the fella who brought sunlight back to my dreary realm." He used his cane to pluck a few more nearby morsels and piled them next to Zeus. "Sit. Eat," Phineus ordered. Zeus did.

Phineus went back to munching his own crumbs. "She was in here just last night, you know," the old hamster said. "Artie, I mean. Took me a moment to recognize her because her hair was so long. Well, that and my eyes were all bedazzled when she conjured the sunlight—like you just did. She was leading some woman around."

"Callie," Zeus said through stuffed cheeks.

"Callie. I didn't catch everything they were saying. I was tucked away in my hidey-hole." Phineus waved vaguely toward a distant pile of tattered crates. "That's where I spend most of my time to avoid the … what'd you call them? Harpies?"

"Yeah," Zeus said, pausing between bites. "What do you

call them?"

"Snatchers. Of course, they huddle in their lair when the lights are on. Smart of you to figure that out. You're a clever lad, Zeus."

Zeus beamed. "Thanks for breakfast … or dinner … or whatever this is," he said, brushing crumbs from his fur. "I know food must be scarce because of the Harpies—er, snatchers."

Phineus smiled weakly. He almost looked … sad. "It's nice to talk to someone for a change. I don't get much company around these parts."

Zeus burped. "Excuse me."

Phineus laughed and poked playfully at the golden thunderbolt emblem on Zeus's chest. "Sounds like you have room for a few more morsels!" He scanned around for more crumbs on the ground, then plucked one with the tip of his cane.

"No, no." Zeus shook his head. "Thanks, but I'm stuffed." He tapped his belly.

"Suit yourself." Phineus stashed the crumb in his beard, and the two sat quietly.

CHAPTER 19

ZEUS FINALLY BROKE THE SILENCE. "I have need of your soothsaying abilities."

"Ah, right," Phineus said. "You mentioned something about a Golden Fleece?"

"Golden *Fleas*," Zeus corrected him.

"*Fleece*," Phineus corrected back.

"Fleece?" Zeus was suddenly confused.

"Well, yeah," Phineus said. "Fleece. Why would any self-respecting hamster want Golden Fleas?" His whiskers twitched. "Makes me itchy just thinking about it."

"Uh, right, Fleece," Zeus said sheepishly. "Of course I meant Fleece. Where can I find the thing?"

Phineus opened his mouth to answer.

"Wait!" Zeus cut him off. "Maybe I want to ask about

the dragon."

"Well, which is it, son? The Fleece or the dragon?"

Zeus's storm cloud rippled. He had wrestled with this decision before. But not in the presence of a soothsayer who could tell him exactly where to find the Golden Fleas—er, Fleece. He still desperately wanted it so he could claim his kingdom—and put an end to Poseidon's maddening disrespect.

But Demeter. She, and everyone in the Bugcropolis, needed rescuing.

Finally, Zeus answered. "The dragon," he said in a small voice.

"Say again? Speak up."

"The dragon," Zeus repeated more confidently.

"That your final answer, son?" Phineus asked.

"It's an answer," Zeus said. "Best one I have for now. The dragon's making trouble for Demeter."

"This Demeter is a close friend?"

"Well, she's a minion," Zeus said. "I'm the king of all the gods, you know."

Phineus nodded.

"She's the goddess of harvests and stuff. That's why she

wears a strip of lettuce across her shoulder. Well, that and she's, like, always hungry."

"I know the feeling." Phineus patted his belly.

"But, yeah, she's also a friend. My best friend. She left the Bugcropolis a long time ago. Showed up outside my palace on Mount Olympus … She was so tired and hungry. She told me she wanted to see the world, so I took her in and made her an Olympian. We've been going on adventures ever since."

"So you feel obligated to help her with this dragon situation." It wasn't a question. Phineus watched Zeus for a moment. "What if you could help your friend *and* obtain the Fleece?"

"Huh?"

"Funny thing about dragons and Golden Fleeces," Phineus said. "Where you find one you often find the other."

Zeus's mouth fell open. "Are you saying they're together?"

"According to the Oracle, the Fleece is guarded by a dragon," Phineus said.

"Really?" Zeus asked. "The Oracle didn't say that. Are

ART TO COME

you sure?"

Phineus poked a thumb at his chest. "Soothsayer."

Zeus stood up and put his paws on Phineus's shoulders. "Do you know what this means, Phineus?" He didn't wait for a reply. "I can help Demeter *and* prove I'm worthy to be king!"

"Some might say those two things go hand in hand."

Zeus wasn't listening. For the first time since leaving Crete, the nagging doubt had left him. He felt like he could accomplish any feat while inspiring his minions. "Okay, Phineus, help me out here: How do I conquer the dragon?"

Phineus stroked his long whiskers. "Well, that depends

on the type of dragon. What did it look like?"

The question surprised the younger hamster. "Don't you know what it looked like? Is this some sort of soothsayer game or something?"

Phineus tapped his cane against Zeus's thunderbolt emblem. "You know we soothsayers don't just hand out easy answers. We speak in riddles and give little quizzes and stuff. It's kind of our thing."

Zeus sighed. He closed his eyes and tried to remember the dragon. "I … I didn't get a good look at it. It ran so fast when Artie accidentally let it out of its lair—"

"Wait, this dragon is the creature Artie released last night?" Phineus interrupted.

"Yeah," Zeus said.

"And it scared the wits out of Artie's friend, uh …"

"Callie," Zeus reminded Phineus.

Phineus began to laugh. Before Zeus could ask what was so funny, the soothsayer said, "Your friend has nothing to fear from this dragon, Zeus."

"She … she doesn't?" Zeus felt lost. "Why not?"

"I heard all about this creature when Artie and her friend came into uncharted territory. Callie was worried that he was on the loose. But then Artie explained why the dragon posed no threat—or, as Artie put it, "wouldn't hurt a fly."

"And why was that?" asked Zeus.

"Because Callie isn't a salad."

"A salad?" Zeus repeated.

"A salad." Phineus nodded, fully satisfied by his soothsayer's riddle.

Zeus sat in mystified silence, puzzling over the answer. Slowly, a grin spread across his face as the meaning of Phineus's words dawned on him. "Well, that's some quality soothsaying, Phineus!"

BOOM!

Both hamsters squeaked as the portal to Greece burst open. Zeus crouched, ready to bolt for cover. But he had no reason to run.

The *Argo* barreled through the portal, driven by Athena with Ares trotting along behind her.

ART TO COME

CHAPTER 20

"**A**THENA! ARES!" ZEUS WHOOPED. "What in blazes are you doing here?"

"We figured out you got trapped in uncharted territory!" Ares shouted. "We're getting you out of here!"

"Boy, am I glad to see you Olympians!" Zeus yelled. He looked beyond the *Argo* at the portal to Greece, which was still slowly swinging open. "Where's Poseidon?"

Athena and Ares exchanged a glance. "We invited him, but, uh … he decided to stay in the Aegean Sea," Athena said.

"Why?" Zeus asked.

Both Ares and Athena looked uncomfortable. Athena

finally spoke. "He said he didn't see the point in helping you when you don't bother to help your own friend."

"Demeter ..." Zeus looked down in shame, his spiky hair drooping over his crown.

Eventually, he remembered the soothsayer standing behind him. "Oh, Olympians, I want you to meet Phineus!" Zeus turned to introduce the old hamster, but he was nowhere in sight.

"Phiney-who?" Ares asked.

"Phineus," Zeus repeated, peering around. "He's a hamster like me, except, like, super old and has terrible fashion sense. He's the soothsayer from the Oracle's tale! I rescued him from the Harpies!"

The Olympians looked around. There was no sign of another hamster.

"I don't understand," Zeus said. "Phineus was just here!"

"Zeus, we don't need a soothsayer," Athena said. "We need you! Demeter's in danger!"

"In danger?" Zeus exclaimed. "What's wrong?" He felt sick. Anything that had happened to Demeter was his fault.

"The dragon's got her!" Ares added. "He chased her all

the way to a super-high-up cliff we can't reach!"

"Take me to them," Zeus ordered. He clambered aboard the *Argo* next to Athena. Phineus was forgotten for the moment. "She'll be okay. I promise."

"I knew you'd know how to rescue her, boss!" said Ares.

"Welcome aboard," said Athena, the owl-shaped charm on her collar twinkling in the bright lights of uncharted territory. "You are now officially an Argonaut."

"I'm kinda overqualified, but okay," Zeus said.

Athena reached out a bracelet-wrapped paw and slapped the button that spurred the *Argo* into motion. "Please keep your paws and tails inside the ship at all times," she said as she brought the vessel about to head back toward the portal to Greece. Ares trotted along behind them.

The Argonauts were just in time to see the portal starting to close.

"Step on it, Athena," Zeus ordered. "Trust me. We do *not* want to get stuck in here."

The *Argo* rolled steadily toward the exit, which was growing alarmingly narrow.

"Faster!" Ares barked.

Athena gestured at the helm's controls. "The *Argo* only has one speed."

"Blast it, Athena!" Zeus shouted. "Raise the main sail! Full steam ahead!

"Yelling that stuff at me won't make any difference," Athena replied. "I'm giving her all she's got!"

"It's not going to be enough." Dread filled Zeus's stomach. They were just a few feet away, but the door was nearly closed. Zeus looked to Athena and back to Ares, padding along behind them, for ideas.

ART TO COME

"Go, go, go, go," Athena muttered under her breath to the *Argo*. Her words reminded Zeus of a time not so long ago when Athena desperately had to *go*. An idea hit him. He looked back again to Ares. "Who's a good boy who wants to go outside?!" he yelled.

The pug shot like a cannonball into the narrowing gap of the portal, his helmet teetering. "Ooh, ooh, ooh, I'm a good boy, Zeus!" he shouted. Ares wriggled himself through the opening and barreled ahead, kicking the portal open behind him. The *Argo* would just make it through.

Ares scampered on to the pug-size portal that led outside until Zeus put two fingers in his mouth and whistled. "Ares! Ares! Get back here!" Ares skidded to a halt and bounded back to the *Argo* with his stubby tail tucked. "Am I still a good boy?" he asked Zeus.

"The best," Zeus replied. "You're the best boy. Now let's go rescue Demeter!"

Ares's tail wagged into overdrive. Athena put the *Argo* in motion. The Argonauts were back in Greece.

CHAPTER 21

AFTER UNCHARTED TERRITORY, GREECE FELT COMFORTING, if shadowy to Zeus. He was relieved to see it was still dark outside. He wasn't sure how much time had passed during his travels, but at least they wouldn't have to worry about Artie returning anytime soon. Familiar landmarks loomed as the *Argo* glided east across the plains of Greece. Despite the urgency of the situation, Zeus was glad to be home.

"What's the plan, boss?" asked Ares as he trotted behind the *Argo*.

"You get me to the dragon and the Fleece, and I'll take

care of the rest," Zeus said.

"The Fleece?" Athena shot Zeus a suspicious look. "Don't you mean Demeter?"

"Right, Demeter, of course," Zeus replied hastily. "Whew. Long night, huh?" He laughed nervously. "So, uh, how'd you guys know I got trapped in uncharted territory?"

"We heard all kinds of scary screeching," Ares said, "so Athena figured we should send in the cavalry." He tapped the side of the *Argo*.

"That Callie lady left the *Argo* docked for us before she and Artie headed out for the night," Athena said. She was still eyeing Zeus carefully.

"Oh, wasn't that nice of her?" Zeus said lightly. "And, uh, how did Demeter end up in the dragon's sights, anyway?"

"She saw that beast bearing down on the Bugcropolis," Ares explained, "so she hopped in front of him as a distraction. She's a hero, Zeus!"

"She lured the dragon away from the Bugcropolis before he could eat her friends," Athena added. "Demeter hopped away for dear life, with the dragon hot on her tail. He followed her east across Greece. All the way up there."

She lifted a paw and pointed.

At the edge of Zeus's vision, high above Greece, Zeus made out a cliff. "All right, well, uh, steady as she goes," he ordered.

The *Argo* rolled past Ares's chambers and Athena's cozy bed. When they reached the Aegean Sea, Athena altered course to veer around its northern edge. Zeus scanned the Aegean for any sign of Poseidon, but the sea lord was nowhere to be seen.

They rode through a canyon crammed with Artie's artifacts. Zeus braced for Ares to take off running when they passed a stack of Mutt Nuggets, but the pug didn't even notice. Finally, the Argonauts reached the far-eastern side of Greece.

"We've arrived," Athena announced as she disengaged the *Argo* and the whir of its motor faded. All three Olympians craned their heads to peer at the cliff high above them. Zeus noticed the first rays of sunlight creeping across Greece. He had been up nearly all night—all the Olympians had—and yet he didn't feel tired. He felt supercharged with excitement.

"What now, boss?" Ares asked.

Zeus set his aegis shield on the deck of the *Argo*. "You two can't fit on this," he explained as he began unspooling its rigid ribbon, "so I'll zip up there and deal with the dragon while you hold down the fort here."

"I can't believe you're gonna face down that dragon all by yourself!" Ares said.

Zeus stopped unspooling the ribbon and puffed up his chest beneath his chiton, the fur on his head standing at attention. "Of course. I'm Zeus the Mighty. Dragons don't scare me."

"What about the Golden Fleece?" Athena demanded.

The question hit Zeus like a slap. "What ... what about the Fleece?"

Ares looked from Athena to Zeus, then lost interest and began biting at an itch on his rump.

"It's pretty obvious the Fleece is still on your mind," Athena said. "Have you really abandoned the quest for it?"

Zeus didn't answer. He was focused on guiding the ribbon to the cliff edge up above. The ribbon became more and more wobbly, and Zeus feared it would topple over. Using every ounce of strength, he guided the ribbon the last few inches until it latched to the cliff edge. *Click.*

"Whew!" Zeus said, shaking out his fatigued fingers. "What were you saying, Athena?"

"You know what I was saying," Athena snapped. "What about the Golden Fleece?"

"Funny thing about dragons and Golden Fleeces," Zeus said as he sat on the shield's boxy seat. "Where you find one you often find the other." He slid the switch.

ZIIIPPP!

Athena and Ares watched Zeus launch skyward.

"What did he mean by that?" Ares asked.

"You got me, war god," Athena replied, "but something tells me we'll find out." She watched Zeus as he shrank to a fuzzy dot above them. "Godspeed, Zeus!"

Unlike the last time he'd ridden the aegis, Zeus was ready for the abrupt stop. He hopped gracefully off, retracted the ribbon, then slipped it on his forearm. He turned to survey the area.

Stacks of crates, no doubt placed up here by Artie, left Zeus with little room to roam. He had nowhere to go except the narrow ledge along the edge of the cliff. It was barely wider than his feet. Zeus put his back to the crates and began shimmying across. Then, he peeked down to see

Ares and Athena watching him from far below. They looked so small, but he could make out the curious expressions on their faces. Zeus leaned out to give a little wave and nearly tumbled forward. "Won't do that again," he mumbled.

Soon Zeus came to what looked like the entrance of a tunnel. Its size and shape reminded him of the dragon's lair near Mount Olympus. Eager to get away from the ledge, Zeus stepped in. The tunnel took a sharp curve to the right. He let his eyes adjust to the dim light, then peeked around the curve. Zeus detected a faint glow from deep inside the tunnel. The exit, perhaps?

A flash of green caught his eye at the end of the tunnel, and Zeus made out the hunched silhouette of a reptile. He double-checked his

ART TO COME

shield, then set off at a run.

Ares and Athena were watching Zeus enter the cave, when a rattle from far across the plains of Greece caught their attention. "Good morning, Olympians!" came a woman's voice. "It's just me, Callie, starting bright and early!"

Ares and Athena looked at each other and ran. They darted around the Aegean Sea to see Artie's friend standing in the portal of Mount Olympus Pet Center. Crouching in the shadows, the two Olympians glanced back up at the high cliff. "Whatever Zeus is doing up there to save Demeter," Athena whispered, "he better do it quickly."

CHAPTER 22

ZEUS CREPT CLOSER AND CLOSER TO THE SHADOWY FORM of the dragon, which sat hunched just outside the tunnel, blocking the exit. Its tail swished slowly back and forth, and it began lowering and lifting itself on its forelegs, doing its strange push-ups again. Zeus was trying to figure out his next move, when he heard a voice.

"I can do this all day, dragon." It was Demeter! She sounded exhausted.

"Demeter!" Zeus's cry startled the dragon. The reptile dashed away from the tunnel's exit, and Zeus took his chance. He came out and found himself in a large clearing that opened on a ledge overlooking all of Greece.

In the middle of the clearing sat a cushion. Demeter

stood on one side, the dragon on the other. Demeter looked tired. Her gilded laurel wreath sat askew on her head. The lettuce sash around her shoulders was tattered.

"Zeus?" Demeter yelled, shocked to see her friend. "What are you doing here?"

"I'm here to save you from the dragon, pal! Are … are you okay?"

"I'm still in one piece," Demeter answered, shifting her eyes back to the dragon, which was flicking its tongue at her across the cushion. "But I'm pretty beat. This beast has been on my tail ever since the Bugcropolis. I … I must've run a hundred laps around this cushion. It's the only thing keeping this monster from gulping me down!"

As if on cue, the dragon darted around the cushion. Demeter scrambled in the opposite direction. "Ssssooo hungry," the dragon hissed, its tongue flicking quickly. "I musssst eat!"

"Yes!" Demeter said. "You must eat. You've only said that a thousand times!"

Zeus took in the situation and noticed the cushion was covered in a plush golden fabric. A picture on its side showed a dozing cat.

ART TO COME

That's when it clicked. In his head, he heard the rousing harp song from the Oracle's stories. "The soothsayer was telling the sooth!" Zeus exclaimed.

"Huh?" Demeter said just as the dragon bolted in the other direction, forcing her to shift again.

"The Golden Fleece!" Zeus exclaimed. "It's here! You found it, Demeter! You found it!"

"I hadn't noticed!" Demeter shouted. "I've been a little busy trying not to get eaten!"

"It's not you he wants to eat!" Zeus declared.

The dragon was circling again. Zeus waited until its back was to him, then lifted his shield and sprinted. He ran up the dragon's tail, across his spiny back, and leapt off its head, landing on the Golden Fleece (so soft!) in between the reptile and Demeter.

"Zeus! Watch out!" Demeter shrieked. "You're as much of a morsel to that beast as I am!"

Zeus put his paw on Demeter's shoulder. "Then I better feed the dragon!" He ripped the lettuce sash from Demeter's chest and held it up in the air.

The dragon's focus immediately shifted to Zeus. "I—I don't understand," Demeter stammered, stepping back from the cushion.

"Fun fact about dragons," Zeus said, locking eyes with the creature. "They're vegetarians. He doesn't want *you*, Demeter—he wants your sash!" With that he hurled the strip of lettuce with all his might. Hissing a loud "yesssss," the dragon caught it in his jaws and devoured it.

Zeus flopped backward onto the Fleece, swishing his arms and legs like he was making a snow angel. "The Fleece! The Fleece! It's all mine!" he shouted excitedly, then sat up and looked at his cricket friend. "Do you know what this means, Demeter?"

She was still staring at the dragon chomping on the lettuce across the clearing. "How ... how'd you know dragons are vegetarians?"

"Phineus the soothsayer told me," Zeus said matter-of-factly. "That guy really knows his stuff."

Demeter looked at Zeus. "But how did you know where to find me?"

"You can thank Athena and Ares for that. They rescued me from the uncharted territory."

"Uncharted territory?" Demeter sounded dazed.

"Yeah," Zeus said, hopping off the Fleece and putting

his arm around Demeter's shoulder. "They rescued me on the *Argo*. It's parked on the plains of Greece. Ares and Athena are down there waiting for you. Come tell them you're okay." Zeus led Demeter to the ledge so she could wave to the other Olympians, but then shot out an arm to stop her.

"Oh no," Zeus said. "What's she doing here?"

Demeter followed Zeus's gaze to see Callie walking toward the portal to uncharted territory.

CHAPTER 23

ARES AND ATHENA WATCHED CALLIE WALK ACROSS GREECE. "Do you think this Callie lady's gonna be coming here every morning?" Ares whispered to Athena, who was crouching in the shadows alongside him.

Athena shrugged.

"I hope so," Ares said. "I like her."

"Huh," Callie said when she reached the portal, which was the slightest bit ajar. "I could've sworn I shut this tight. I hope that crazy cat didn't get into my tools again." She pushed the door completely open.

SCREEEEEEEE!

"Aiieee!" Callie squealed. She found herself surrounded

by flying creatures with leathery wings. They swarmed above her and into the pet center, which was still dim in the light of dawn.

Ares and Athena watched the cloud of black creatures swirling over their heads. "Those must be the Harpies Zeus was telling us about," Athena said. "Heads up, Zeus!" she called to him. "Your friends are paying Greece a visit!"

Zeus didn't need Athena's warning. From their ledge, he saw the cloud of Harpies heading toward them. "Aw, I hate these guys," Zeus muttered, then yelled, "Demeter, take cover!"

Zeus raised the aegis shield and deflected the claws of a diving Harpy, giving Demeter time to bolt for the safety of the tunnel. Zeus turned to follow but found the dragon in front of him, blocking the tunnel's entrance. The Harpies had the dragon in a panic. He spun and lashed his tail. Zeus dove behind the Golden Fleece for cover, but it was the wrong move. The dragon's next tail swish slapped the Fleece into Zeus and knocked them both off the ledge.

Zeus plummeted toward the plains of Greece. He braced for impact, expecting the hard ground to rush up and meet him any second. His last thought was for Demeter.

ART TO COME

He smiled, knowing she had made it to the safety of the tunnel.

Splash!

Zeus came up sputtering salty water. He had landed in the Aegean Sea! He looked up in time to see the Golden Fleece slam into the water next to him. It bobbed on the surface for a moment, then listed and began to sink. "No!" Zeus shouted, grabbing it. But the waterlogged Fleece was like an anchor. Zeus couldn't keep it afloat.

He was having a hard time keeping himself above water as it was. It seemed to be rising around him, stinging his eyes. No matter how hard he kicked, he kept sinking. Almost as though something was tugging him underwater. His shield!

Zeus jerked his arm, but he couldn't free himself from the aegis's clip. He succeeded only in making himself more exhausted. As he went under a final time, a blurry vision rose in front of him. Something *big*, with see-through skin. It looked ready to swallow him. Zeus released the last of his air.

About to pass out, he felt a sudden flood of bubbles around him. Air? He sucked in a deep breath. The air tasted rubbery, but sweet—the sweetest breath he ever took. Zeus coughed up water and slowly realized where he was: inside Poseidon's dive helmet on the bottom of the Aegean Sea. Poseidon's minions hadn't filled it with water like usual, so Zeus was sealed inside, safely surrounded with air.

Tink! Tink! Zeus jumped at the sound of something knocking on the helmet. He looked up to see Poseidon brandishing his trident just outside the helmet. Next to him, drifting in the current, was the Golden Fleece. "Looking for this?" Poseidon asked, his voice echoey and faint through the helmet.

Zeus tried to respond but was racked by a fit of coughing. Water sprayed from his mouth. He sank to the floor, gasping.

"Hey, you okay in there, Zeus?" Poseidon shouted. He turned to his seahorse minions who were holding the air-filled helmet to the seafloor. "Let's get him to the surface, lads!"

CHAPTER 24

ARTIE HAD AN EASY COMMUTE TO MOUNT **OLYMPUS PET CENTER**—she lived across the street. She arrived every day at 8 a.m., which gave her an hour to feed and play with the animals and maybe listen to a *Greeking Out* podcast before she opened the shop. Today was no different, although she was surprised to find the front door unlocked.

"Um, hello? Callie?" she called, peeking into the dark interior. A flurry of black creatures blasted past her, tussling her hair and filling her ears with a chorus of screeches. They immediately disappeared, rising into the sky like a black cloud.

Stunned, Artie stepped into the shop and let the door

close behind her. She looked around, ready for anything, but the only other creature she saw stirring was Callie standing by the door to the expansion, a look of shock on her face. "Morning, Artie," she said, sounding robotic.

"Good morning," Artie replied. "Sooo, where did those bats come from?"

"In there," Callie murmured, pointing to uncharted territory.

"Okay," Artie said. "Well, thanks for letting them out." She added quickly, "They weren't mine, by the way."

Callie visibly relaxed, and then laughed. "I guess you did warn me there'd be monsters."

CRASH!

"Oh, what now?" Artie said. A display of cat-scratching posts had toppled to the floor. She raced over to find a green reptile squatting atop the pile. "Kiko!" Artie cried. "Where'd you come from?" She reached down and scooped the iguana up before he could scramble away again.

"What, did he fall from the sky?" Callie asked.

"Maybe," Artie laughed. "Green iguanas are really good climbers. They can get into pretty much anything."

"Oh, how wonderful for them," Callie said sarcastically.

"I think I'll stick with dogs and cats."

Artie carried the animal back to his crate and secured him inside. "There you go, Kiko. I'll go make you a nice salad. I bet you're starving!"

"Speaking of dogs, where's my buddy Ares?" Callie asked, crossing to the front of the store. She was passing the aquarium tanks, when something caught her eye. "Artie, quick! Come here!"

Artie rushed over to find her favorite hamster sealed inside a toy diving helmet. "Zeus!" She plucked his limp body out of the helmet and held him close to her face, checking to see if he was breathing. She pressed on his chest with a finger. "Zeus, wake up! Zeus!" She pressed again.

Zeus sputtered, coughing up water. Artie rolled him onto his stomach, and he spit up more. "That's right, little guy," Artie said, sounding relieved. "Get it all out."

"Is that … Is that my tape measure at the bottom of that tank?" Callie asked. She was about to retrieve it when she saw a sparkle of gold. "What's that?" She pulled out a soggy cushion.

Artie glanced at the object in Callie's hand. "Ah, that's one of our best-selling cat beds," she said. "How'd it wind up in the tank, I wonder? And how in the world did you find your way into this helmet?" she asked Zeus. Artie set the helmet on the floor, and Callie used it to catch the water she wrung out of the sodden Fleece.

Ares suddenly appeared out of and started lapping up the Fleece water from the dive helmet. "Blech! Yuck!" he spit water everywhere.

"Hey, that's salt water, silly," Artie said, grabbing the helmet from Ares and dropping it back in the aquarium.

"Honestly, watching a dog drink from a deep-sea helmet is the least weird thing I've seen in the last five

ART TO COME

minutes," Callie said. She held up the cat bed to inspect it.

Zeus coughed up the last of the water and rubbed the stinging salt water from his eyes—which went wide when he saw Callie. The storm cloud on his cheek quivered. "The Fleece! Oh no, Callie found the Fleece!" How would he claim his kingdom now?

"Come on, little guy," Artie said, still cradling Zeus. "Let me get you dried off." She wrapped the hamster in a rag. Zeus squirmed and squeaked. Artie lifted him up to his cage on its high shelf. "Back to Mount Olympus you go." She laid him gently inside on his little hamster bed.

Zeus thought about racing to the columns of his palace to see where Callie would take the Fleece—but the bed just felt so cozy. The night's adventure had finally caught up with him. Zeus curled into a ball and fell asleep.

ART TO COME

Callie watched Artie checking on her other animals. "Something tells me every day is going to be an adventure around here," Callie said. "So what do you want me to start on first in your uncharted territory?" she asked. "Want me to dismantle those shelves or uncover the windows or—"

"Actually," Artie interrupted, "could you fix the shop's toilet so it'll stop running all the time? I'm worried one of the critters'll drown in that thing."

"No problem." Callie walked to her bag and dug out a plunger. "Yep, every day's an adventure."

CHAPTER 25

ZEUS THE MIGHTY WOKE FEELING STIFF AND SORE. Greece was dark. He had slept the entire day.

"Was it all a dream?"

"Nope," a familiar voice answered. "At least I hope not."

"Demeter?!" Zeus shouted. His friend was lounging in Zeus's exercise wheel, nibbling on a fresh strip of lettuce. Zeus could hardly believe his eyes. He ran to the cricket and scooped her up, hugging her so tightly that Demeter's eyes bulged.

"Hey, ha-ha, easy," she said, laughing and squirming. "We Bugcropolis types don't do well with being squished, you know."

Zeus looked the cricket up and down. "You're okay?

The Harpies didn't get you?"

"Kiko actually kept them away from me."

"Kiko?" Zeus repeated.

"Yeah, the dragon. We're kind of pals now, if you can believe that. And to think I thought Kiko wanted to eat me!" Demeter laughed. After a moment, she said, "Thank you, Zeus, for coming to my rescue."

Zeus looked down. "It was the least I could do."

"No, no, no! You gave up your quest for the Golden Fleece to come after me. That's about the most you could do."

"I'm sorry I didn't do it sooner," Zeus said solemnly, "and I'm sorry I didn't believe you about the dragon."

"Hey, because of you, we know the dragon's not a danger now. Heck, you even took a dip in the Aegean Sea because of me. And I know how much you hate pruny fingers!"

Zeus laughed and rubbed his paws together. "It was all worth it. I'm just glad you're okay. Who needs a furry old Fleece anyway?"

"Ah, ah, ah." Demeter wagged an arm. "You sure about that?" She pointed to the ledge outside the palace. There

sat the Golden Fleece, still damp, but intact.

"The Fleece!" Zeus exclaimed.

"Callie set it up here to dry," Demeter said. "She said she figured you'd like a big bed after your misadventure."

"This means … I can claim my throne! I can rule Greece!" Zeus said. "I'm worthy to be your king!"

"Of course you are," said Demeter. "You're Zeus the Mighty."

"Hey, Zeus, you alive up there?" a voice called.

"Athena!" Zeus ran to the edge of his palace and peered down. Not just Athena, but all of the Olympians, had gathered at the foot of Mount Olympus. Poseidon (in his helmet) sat atop the *Argo* with Athena. Ares sat nearby scratching at an ear beneath his bronze helmet.

"The night's young," Athena called. The owl charm on her collar sparkled red in the light cast by the Mount Olympus Pet Center sign. "We thought you might be up for a little adventure."

Zeus turned to Demeter. "You coming, buddy?"

I've had enough fun for one week. You run along. I'll hold down the fort."

Zeus nodded. "Wait for me, guys! I'll be right there!" He remembered that he'd lost the aegis in the Aegean Sea. Too bad; he could've made a dramatic entrance.

"Looking for this, Zeus?" Poseidon called. The sea lord had the silver shield balanced on top of his helmet. "My minions retrieved it for you."

Zeus whooped and slid down the rope of his cage to the foot of Mount Olympus, where he hopped aboard the *Argo*. He plucked the aegis off Poseidon's helmet and put it on his forearm. "Thanks, Poseidon!"

"Think nothing of it, Zeus," Poseidon said. "That was some inspiring work with the dragon, you know. I dare say you've earned the right to rule."

"Really?" Zeus said.

"On dry land, of course," Poseidon clarified. "The Aegean Sea is still my realm." He tapped his crown with his trident.

Zeus was in too good a mood to argue.

"Oh, I kept this safe for you," Athena said, patting Hekate's torch beside her. "It makes a great headlight for the *Argo*!"

Zeus reached down and switched it on.

"So where to, King?" Athena asked.

"You're the captain," Zeus replied. "You set our course."

"If you say so. Thanks, Zeus." Athena pawed the big circular button that brought the *Argo* to life. "Let's go see if we can chart some of that uncharted territory!"

Zeus, Athena, and the rest of the Argonauts headed toward the edge of the known world, eager to begin a new quest.

BACKMATTER:
The Truth Behind the Fiction

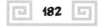

BACKMATTER:
The Truth Behind the Fiction

BACKMATTER:
The Truth Behind the Fiction

BACKMATTER:
The Truth Behind the Fiction

BACKMATTER:
The Truth Behind the Fiction

BACKMATTER:
The Truth Behind the Fiction

SNEAK PEEK:
Zeus 2

SNEAK PEEK:
Zeus 2

SNEAK PEEK:
Zeus 2

SNEAK PEEK:
Zeus 2

ACKNOWLEDGMENTS